The
Secret Library

Essential sensual reading

Silk Stockings

3 sensual novellas

Silk Stockings
by Constance Munday

The Lord of Summer
by Jenna Bright

Off the Shelf
by Lucy Felthouse

Silk Stockings – Constance Munday

When Michael Levenstein meets Imogen, an exotic dancer at a Berlin nightclub, a passionate and intense love story develops. Michael becomes obsessed by mysterious Imogen and falls into a world of intense sexual fantasy and desire. But Imogen is determined to protect a personal, dark secret at all costs and because of this she has forbidden herself love.

With Imogen afraid of committing and afraid of losing what she has fought for so desperately, can Michael break down her barriers and discover a solution to his lover's deep dark secret, thus freeing the enigmatic Imogen to truly love him?

The Lord of Summer – Jenna Bright

Banished to the back of beyond, in the middle of a long, hot summer, Gem and Dan Parker find their marriage filling up with secrets. As they work to reopen the Green Man pub, tensions and unacknowledged desires come between them. From their first night, when Gem sees someone watching them make love from the edge of the woods, her fantasies of having two men at once start to grow and consume her. As the temperature rises, she becomes fixated by her imaginings of an impossible, gorgeous, otherworldly man in the forest. A man who could make her dreams come true – and maybe save her marriage.

Off the Shelf – Lucy Felthouse

At 35, travel writer Annalise is fed up with insensitive comments about being left "on the shelf". It's not as if she doesn't *want* a man, but her busy career doesn't leave her much time for relationships. Sexy liaisons with passing acquaintances give Annalise physical satisfaction but she needs more than that. She wants a man who will satisfy her mind as well as her body. But where will she find someone like that?

It seems Annalise may be in luck when a new member of staff starts working in the bookshop at the airport she regularly travels through. Damien appears to tick all the boxes – he's gorgeous, funny and intelligent, and he shares Annalise's love of books and travel.

The trouble is, Damien's shy and Annalise is terrified of rejection. Can they overcome their fears and admit their feelings, or are they doomed to remain on the shelf?

Published by Xcite Books Ltd – 2012
ISBN 9781908262042

Cover design by Madamadari

Contents

www.xcitebooks.com

Scan the QR code to join our mailing list

More great titles in
The Secret Library

Traded Innocence
9781908262028

One Long Hot Summer
9781908262066

The Thousand and One Nights
9781908262080

The Game
9781908262103

Hungarian Rhapsody
9781908262127

Silk Stockings
by Constance Munday

Chapter One

THE NIGHT IMOGEN MET Michael Levenstein, she was sitting at the bar wearing a fashionably short skirt, a pair of impossibly high stiletto heels and she was sipping a cocktail.

It had been a bad idea coming here, because men frequently followed her out of the club; men and boys, who assumed just because she was an exotic dancer, they had a divine right over her legs. The boys followed her in groups sometimes with their hands in their pockets walking right behind her and talking too loudly and making comments and whistling; the older men, studying the back of her legs like a cat studies a bird in the grass, tensing up ready to pounce. Already, that night, some guy had come too close to her and put his hand on her thigh and it irritated her, the way they always seemed to be touching her up or thinking about touching her up. Just because she had these damn legs, yes, this curse of a pair of legs.

Early on when she was 17 she'd learnt that, although not a show-stopper, she was a passably pretty fräulein and men gazed at her because Imogen had other more enviable attributes; she oozed sex, she oozed it from every pore. She'd always been a bit too fond of butterkuchen and when she was a child Imogen had constantly been caught with her fingers in the cake bowl, or stealing one of her grandma's honey cakes to feed her insatiable appetite. This had given her an exceedingly attractive, softly rounded body with plump arms and legs, and ample hips. It was when she sat down or bent over though, that you really noticed that the show-stoppers were her legs, which she had inherited from her mother – the silk stocking whore. Guys had been known to jerk off on street corners looking at Imogen's legs and simply the sight of her leaning against a park bench easing out the creases in a pair of her fine silk stockings was enough to get them panting like rutting dogs.

On the day, quite some time ago, when she walked into the Blue Palm Club for the job, Luther said he'd never seen a girl like Imogen. He said she had jerk-off legs, a particularly powerful destructive weapon which were capable of some kind of erotic conjuration. Luther had seen a lot of women in his time but Imogen's legs turned his insides to water.

'Hitch up your skirt and put your foot on that chair,' Luther asked. Imogen did so.

'Now move around a bit.'

She wasn't a trained dancer at all, in fact, up until that point in her life, she'd never done a dance class but Imogen had an easy, show girl way of walking with a forward thrusting gait which was very sexy and she could pose exotically, not unlike a hooker, tantalising the audience by crossing and uncrossing her legs and occasionally touching them with her long red fingernails. When Imogen came along Luther's takings went up by 70 per cent. Well, every guy enjoyed looking at a silk stocking whore. Often, men came up to her and whispered things in her ear such as, "hey, how about I cream your legs, your fabulous fucking legs," or, "Liebchen, I want to get down on my knees and worship your hose and next I want to lick you all over."

Michael Levenstein wore a nice light wool suit and he didn't have the hard-bitten look of most of the guys who frequented Larry's bar and that was what captured Imogen's attention. Now, if I wanted a boyfriend, that's the kind of man I'd go for, she speculated. He had smoothly rounded Nordic cheeks and unruly hair which he kept running his hands through, it was his eyes though which melted her. Michael's emerald green eyes were as much show-stoppers as Imogen's legs.

She stirred her drink with her finger. Goddamnit, now he was looking at her legs. Ah well, it was a fact of life. Her mama would have warned her about Michael's kind. He was what Mama would have called smooth, as smooth as the best pair of silk stockings; a man too attractive and pretty for his own good. Well, it hardly mattered since she wasn't in the market for romance. Imogen had learnt how to instantly size up men. It came from a strong sense of self-preservation and living when she was younger like a tramp and having men continually coming up to her and cornering her so that they could slide a hand under her skirt and feel her silk stockings.

She stroked the stem of her glass in the suggestive way she might stroke a man's cock and then she uncrossed her legs. Her heart was beginning to beat a little bit faster like a butterfly against the wings of a jar. That was another thing her mother had warned her about. Be careful you don't beat your wings too hard against that glass illusion, 'cause one day you're gonna hurt yourself. Christ knows she couldn't afford the danger of a love affair although, a quick hard fuck to appease this gnawing frustration would be good.

Michael Levenstein must have been thinking of something amusing, because he was smiling and the smile was crinkling the scattering of lines at the corner of his eyes. He had the look of a man who had been stung by a savage wasp and she knew the look well. It was as if his eyes had become magnets and they were attracted to the opposing magnet of her legs and now that irresistible force was steering him to look again. He was fighting it and it amused her to watch him resist that attraction, as he watered his scotch down a bit more and glanced at her in the mirror over

3

the bar.

Imogen experienced the stirring of something she hadn't felt in a long time and it was real jaw-crunching desire. The more he looked at her, the more she was considering how much she'd like to fuck him and to hell with the consequences.

As if making a sudden decision, he loosened his smart tie and the top button of his crisp, starched white shirt and, slithering off his stool, Michael Levenstein walked unsteadily and as if a little drunk across the room towards her, before passing directly by her and through the door at the end. That room led to one place and one place only, it led into the men's washroom and she wondered if he'd gone in there to jerk off. Men often jerked off after they'd spent a while or so considering her legs and she found it crass and a little unbelievable how shallow a man could be in that respect. You never saw a woman eyeing a man's cock and then slithering off a stool and going to the powder room for a gratifying orgasm, or – she pressed her hand to her mouth, to stop a giggle – perhaps you did.

Imogen picked up her packet of cigarettes and turning it around in her hand she shook one through the tiny hole she'd made in the end of the packet and she watched it ease out like a kind of "hard-on" cigarette, before pushing it back with the tip of her finger like she might a man's belligerent cock. 'Hey, get back in there where you belong. I sure as shit gave you up and I'm not reneging on that promise to Anni.' She'd promised a lot of things to Anni and somehow she meant to deliver. For instance, a nice apartment overlooking the park, pretty clothes and shoes and a little holiday.

By now Imogen hazarded a guess that Michael was in the washroom splashing water on his face, loosening his tie a bit more, even taking it off maybe and putting it in his pant's pocket, and next unfastening the top button of his shirt as he stared glassy-eyed into the mirror above the wash basin.

"Yes, I know," he'd say to his reflection. "It's crazy to be so turned on and seduced by a woman in a pair of silk stockings and there's no logical explanation for it. But boy I never saw a broad who could wear a pair of stockings with such panache and make them such a powerful sexual tool."

She hoped Michael would go to the john right at the end of the row, because then he'd have the big surprise that all the guys remarked over. He'd see the picture on the wall done by the famous artist, Jake de la Mare, who took a great interest in painting the more intimate parts of a woman's body. Yes, that Jake, the one that only six months after saying he wanted to fuck her all over her pretty legs had boldly gone to New York with his unique portfolio and been offered a first exhibition on the strength of it and was now doing illustrations for some big time magazines and PR companies. Jake had never tried to fuck her but he liked her and Jake was a decent guy. He'd never said he loved her per se, however, he'd been the first guy she'd connected with since Louis and she'd had good times with Jake. When she turned down the job as his model, Jake said he would leave the world an enduring memento and he'd painted the picture and left it on the john wall – so as he put it – the whole of the male population of Berlin could share the dream boat pair of legs and not have to fantasise so hard about her when they jerked off. She'd liked Jake, Jake had been nice to her and he'd talked about her legs like they were assets, which in a way they were, and he'd joked about her job at the club, which made her feel better for doing it.

Larry hated guys dirtying up his john and he boasted he had one of the cleanest johns in Berlin, but this time when he went in with his bucket and scrubbing brush he came straight back out again. 'I'm not scrubbing it out, Imogen, 'cause it's a rather fine piece of work. Come and look at it.'

'I already did,' she said. Imogen knew about the painting, because Jake had sneaked her into the john and he'd showed her the picture before asking if he could have a last feel of the silk stockings for old times sake. For some reason it never aggravated her that Jake wanted to see a show of the stockings, and putting her foot on the seat of the john, she'd done a private striptease in the cubicle for Jake, peeling the silk stocking down ever so slowly while he took out his dick and fiddled with it. Then, she hung one of her silk stockings around his neck and carefully tied it like she used to tie Louis's tie when he went out to work, tapped it with her finger and kissed him on the cheek. Jake had laughed. 'I got to confess, baby, I have wet dreams about your legs. I'd like to press my nose up to those silk stockings and eat my way into your pussy, 'cause you'd have to experience sex with the girl in the silk stockings to know what sure as shit ecstasy is.'

Was Michael Levenstein fiddling with his dick right now? Did he have his pants down around his ankles as he conjured his cock into life, fantasising about her and wondering how to engage the cold dame with the hard eyes into life? Well, it wouldn't be easy. Imogen had built a mighty fine wall around herself and it would take a lot of constant chipping at the brickwork to get through. Perhaps if he made her upset her glass of wine, the wine would stain those fine stockings and she'd go to the powder room and remove them? It was unlikely she'd throw them in the trash because they seemed expensive, but, probably she'd place them in her purse and if she did and she left that purse lying on the counter – he was sure he could dream up some way to open it and steal them. My God, by imagining he could even stoop as low as to steal a pair of women's hose, he'd have dropped to the sleaziest level possible and he'd be thinking like a pervert, but all men were perverts in one way or another, and especially if they were crazed by sexual obsession. Imogen would have easily given him a pair of the silk stockings though, because she liked him. When she went home that evening she might even open her chest of drawers, full of silk stockings, and think which of them

6

would suit him and how best he would choose to use them.

Lover's fantasies, Imogen thought sadly, as she snapped back into the present. They were as easy to slip into as slipping on a shoe, but dangerous just for that reason. She wondered if sex came back to you like riding a bicycle or if a woman's insides dried up like a poorly oiled machine from lack of use. What was it they said? "Use it or lose it!" Either that or it would be better for the period of abstinence, and when a man began to fuck her, she'd be so much fire she'd scorch him to a crisp. Her mind waded into deeper and progressively more dangerous waters. Michael had sexy lips and those type of lips made a man good at kissing, they were fine cunt kissing lips. Firstly, he'd kiss her on her lips and then on her nipples and a little bit later on when she was more relaxed and warm, he'd perhaps kiss her on her secret places; between her ample but firm butt cheeks and in her cunt.

Chapter Two

IMOGEN WAS THINKING OF all these things when Michael came out of the john and with a curious shiver she realised he must indeed have been in the one at the end, because he was very flushed and perspiring a little while his eyes gleamed with a feverish light.

Michael returned to his stool at the other end of the bar and then thinking for a moment he dragged it closer to hers until he was almost within touching distance. Of course, it was essential he got closer so he could look at the silk stockings, which were gleaming enticingly in the dim light of the bar and which Imogen had now boldly crossed.

It wasn't unusual to see a woman in stockings – but there was something about the way she wore them. It was as if she was made to wear a pair of hose in the way some girls are made to wear gloves or pearls. There was no doubt the silk stockings and the woman were a uniquely erotic combination and no other woman on the planet could carry off such a stunning partnership.

Imogen watched Michael for several minutes and before she realised what she was doing, she speared him with her cheeky gaze and raising her glass she invited a toast. It was something she never did and there was a steely determination in her glance, not unlike a whore's invitation, but in a way she was a whore. She was, as Louis had so quaintly put it, the silk stocking whore – a cocktease in Cervin.

Michael smiled at her. She hazarded a guess he was doing what most men did, he was wondering if she had a boyfriend or if she was a high class whore waiting for a punter since she seemed expectant and her gaze kept continually darting to the door. The truth of the matter was, though, Imogen couldn't get rid of the irrational fear which seemed to be mounting up inside her day by day, the fear Louis would walk right back in and blackmail her.

After awhile Imogen fished an olive out of her drink and popping it between her lips she dried her finger on her thigh. She didn't mean to do it, but the action of the finger drew Michael's attention to the silk stockings. She rubbed her finger up and down suggestively and then she drew several small circles on her thigh before hitching her skirt skilfully up her legs. She didn't want to tempt him but she couldn't help it, she liked him. She liked his wide-eyed innocent look and his slim sexy physique and narrow hips. He was American, she'd guessed that immediately because he talked with a bit of a twang like Jake, but Jake had a broad Brooklyn accent and Michael's accent was soft and husky as if he'd just had sex and rolled out of bed. Even that voice was enough to get her going for some reason. It sent shivers all the way up her spine.

Michael travelled the world in his high powered job as top sales executive in his sister-in-law's cosmetic firm. He was a rebel like his father and he'd been groomed to walk in Abel Levenstein's shoes, but when he left law school Michael found, although he had a certain genius just like his father for law, he didn't want to be a facsimile of a legal Levenstein.

Being a famous Levenstein wasn't easy and when he dropped the bombshell, Abel didn't talk to him for six months, but the family were close and a compromise was reached. He now employed his skills to good use in Marta's employ. He enjoyed selling useful products and he could put his legal skills to good use. Furthermore, he loved the job because he was constantly meeting and able to appraise stunning women, women of incredible and outstanding beauty. He'd been to many exotic countries and he'd shared a bed with a fair quantity of fascinating girls. Girls he had to admit, who were exceedingly enchanting and sexually provocative and sometimes had eclectic and surprising sexual repertoires but whose beautiful flawless looks became in a while just a little bit repetitive. In all those bars, in all those hotels, he'd never seen a dame as exciting as Imogen, the woman in the silk stockings.

Michael was also not a hustler and he didn't behave like a lot of guys who hopped in out of bed with every broad who approached them. No. He liked to experience some kind of enchantment and be attracted to a woman in more than the base physical way before he went to bed with her. What's more, he'd never gone for orthodox beauty. He enjoyed having his interest piqued by something exceptional. This time, shockingly, it was the enchantment of Imogen's incredible sex tools in the silk stockings.

Michael was astute, he'd been trained as a lawyer after all, and in a few seconds he'd sized Imogen up. He liked her thick natural blonde hair, which Imogen had piled stylishly high on top of her head and which was fastened with two tortoiseshell combs, and he liked the way the hair which was swept away from her cheeks, accentuated her lustrous blue eyes.

At that precise moment Hermann Meier, who was fresh out of a club with his latest mistress, came into the bar shaking raindrops off his coat and then, taking his hat off and shaking that too, he left the woman sitting at a table and noticing Imogen came over to her. 'Looking good as always,' he said gruffly. 'Boy, you were so hot tonight you were sizzling.'

Imogen laughed. Meier had power in the Berlin entertainments industry. He scouted clubs such as her one, and recruited women for his special photographic sessions. He was well known for his daring photography, which some said verged on the pornographic, but being daring got his models noticed. Some had become stars and even ended up in the movie industry in Hollywood, a fact which Hermann had made plain to Imogen. Sure, he could make her a star too. She didn't need to think about it twice though and she'd turned him down. A public profile didn't suit her and the fear welled up like a volcano, but Meier never gave up, he knew something special when he saw it. Meier, who was also obsessed by her legs, was staring at her stockings and looking her up and down.

'Thought I'd find you here, why the shit do you still come into this sleazy joint?' Imogen shrugged, she had a very good reason. How could she tell Meier, indeed, how could she tell anyone, about the fear which constantly licked at her heels and nibbled away at the fringes of her tattered nerves? The fear that, one evening, that shadow would come closer and she would go home and find another plain brown envelope pushed under her door. It was bad enough having to go home at all, to face the cold apartment which was really little more than a single room and where the wind whistled between the cracks. She hated it, with its smell of cabbage and the constant thump of Frieda the whore as she pounded the floor above her. Her only escape was thinking of Anni, Anni wrapped up in her snug little room at Helga Streiber's.

'You realise I could still make you that huge star, cookie? Just think about it, a fraction of the work and 50 times more dough. I'm determined I can wear you down and you'll see sense.'

Imogen's attention snapped back to the present. 'Don't I know it, Hermann and you know the answer to that.' She was distracted: she still had her eye on Michael, who was watching her quizzically

Imogen felt warm drenching feelings of sexual arousal start as Michael stared at the silk stockings. She hoped Michael was dreaming of placing his finger on the cool silk and rubbing it between his fingertips, because for once she

11

thought she'd like that rather a lot.

'What's the matter with you? You look goddamned distracted. You got a boyfriend?'

'Hermann, when would I have the time for a boyfriend? Besides, you know I don't date.'

'Sure, sure I do. Cold fish ain't you?' He stroked her cheek and Imogen smiled, she was fizzing from the tips of her toes to the roots of her hair and her heart was beating like an African tribal drum. She wanted to tantalise Michael, she thought as she darted a glance at his bowed head. For the first time in ages she wanted to feel his finger coming up her exquisitely shaped thigh and she wanted to feel herself contracting her strong thigh muscles around his hand as he sunk his fingers inside her and they built up some skin on skin friction. Then she fantasised over how she'd drive him crazy in bed, dressed only in the silk stockings and how the abrasive friction provided by her stockings against his legs and cock – as he pumped in and out of her warm woman's glove – would make him roar like a lion.

Hermann put his hand on her thigh. For some reason when he put his hand there she never felt it was offensive. Naturally, he wanted to stroke her legs in her expensive silk stockings, all guys did. In fact, the legs and the stockings created a scene of such erotic perfection the need to do it was overpowering.

'Shit, there's no other woman on the planet who can make a pair of silk stockings look like you do, you take a man to jerk off heaven. You know, babe, I've puzzled and puzzled over it. I mean a lot of dames look good in hose, and, hell, I've seen a million dames in silk stockings, but you, God it's weird and I still can't figure out that weird alchemical magic you got going. Those goddamn stockings cling to your legs as if it's all one thing and made to go together, you know like strawberries and cream or, Fred Astaire and Ginger Rogers.' He rubbed his chin. 'Now, babe, if you got that kind of magic, why don't you milk it, why don't you make a million from it? That's what I can't understand!'

'I told you, I got my reasons.'

Hermann nodded. 'You got balls of steel, you know that. Whatever it is that drives you, honey, I'd sure like to know what it is? I'll be seeing you, babe.'

'Sure, Hermann.'

'And, I'm gonna break you down, babe.'

'I doubt that.'

Hermann left and Michael, seeing his opportunity, pulled his stool even closer to the irresistible silk force, while Imogen studied him cautiously out of the corner of her eye.

He had a gentle smooth face and his long, brushed back hair folded carelessly around the collar of his shirt. She felt a wave of lust, a hot shafting pulse of desire.

'Hi,' Michael said, without looking at her. 'You seem to have been waiting here a long time. Can I buy you another drink?'

The warm jolt fizzed through her like electricity; she liked to be engaged in the thought of love.

'I'm not a whore, you know!' There was more than a hint of sarcasm added as a final drop of poison to her words. 'I'm a respectable girl, in case you wondered. If you want a whore you can go to some other place, Berlin's full of them.'

Her voice possessed a mellifluous quality embellished with a husky undertone; she had a thick German accent but spoke fluid English, her mother having insisted on it. Her mother had wanted Imogen to have every advantage. She'd had a nice apartment and sent Imogen to a good school.

Michael's fingers moved tirelessly, stroking his fine wool pants as, occasionally, he glanced at her legs. Yes, he had that strange affliction most men had, she thought with amusement, he was determined to pursue his quest of touching the silk stockings and he was wondering how close he could get.

She twisted around a little on the bar stool and flexing her foot she rested it back on the footrest. She was deliberately teasing him. Beneath the silk she wore a small silver bracelet around her slim little ankle. She knew it looked tacky and gave her the appearance of a whore, but Jake had given it to her and she liked to be a little bit wicked after all. She wanted to see how hard men would stare at the silk stockings as they imagined peeling down the silk to look at her bare legs.

'You seem to be waiting for someone?' Michael commented.

'What if I am? It's nothing to do with you, is it? Can't a girl sit quietly and listen to some music and have a nice drink without being continually bothered.'

'Yes, they can,' Michael replied. 'But not if they're a girl in a pair of silk stockings.' He evidently thought this was funny because he was smiling. 'You have to see it from a guy's point of view. A beautiful woman sitting alone is bound to arouse speculation.'

'Maybe I've been stood up.'

'Maybe, you have.'

She ran her finger through a pile of sugar on the counter before touching it to her lips. 'Or, possibly I'm lying to you and I really am a whore after all, and I'm waiting for a punter. You don't know a fuck about me!' Running her tongue over her full painted lips she hitched herself further onto the stool and as she did so, she crossed and uncrossed her legs with the delicious hissing crackle of static electricity. It would be possible for a pair of sexy legs to issue an electrical spark.

Her gaze roamed over him and something stirred which was very exciting

Beneath the nicely tailored pair of pants which fit like a glove and said money, money, money, his cock was thick and ropey and she could see it rising up, straining for attention.

'I used to act tough like you,' he said expectantly, while he sipped his scotch and waited for a verbal counter attack from her – a wild spray of her angry words like rogue bullets. 'But, it wasted too much energy. It's better to channel that energy into something useful, like solving the reason why you're so shit angry at the world in the first place.'

Imogen pushed her packet of cigarettes around the bar top, then she glanced at her watch. 'Who the fuck said I was angry at the world?'

'You didn't have to, it's written all over your face.' His voice was soft and kind and maybe concerned. 'It's either that or you're scared shitless of something.'

Imogen bit her lip. He was astute and his eyes seemed to look deep inside her, she sat back on her stool and uncrossed her legs.

'Whoever this guy is, who's causing so much hassle, it looks like he's not showing,' Michael said jokingly. Then his gaze drifted to her legs. 'You remind me of my mother. She had great legs like yours, all the guys looked at her legs. My father thought legs were ten times more erotic than breasts.'

'Is that the only reason you came over to talk to me? Because my sexy silk stocking legs reminded you of your mother and made you horny?' Imogen stated acerbically.

'No, no,' Michael stuttered. 'Of course not. Shit, I always put my foot in it with ladies.'

'Cut to the chase,' she said, spurred on by the wicked sex devil inside her. 'You want to fuck me, so say so. Why don't we go outside and I'll take off these damn silk stockings and you'll see these legs are not as perfect and so much of a wet dream as you think. Perhaps you fancy fucking me up against the wall?'

Imogen couldn't help herself; she was being deliberately provocative for some reason. The tender stirring, the need for physical comfort was making her run off at the mouth. It wasn't like her, not like her at all. 'Perhaps, you want to watch me pull them on and off very slowly and then fuck me in them. Is that it, huh? Or, maybe you'd like to see me stripped naked and just dressed in the hose? It's hardly surprising since I make my living from these fucking legs.'

Michael grinned at her. 'Boy, hold on a moment. Who rattled your cage?'

Imogen was about to say, "You did! You walked too close and you put your face right up to the bars and despite the fact I fluttered my wings a little in warning, you persisted and now I've struck out and pecked you with my sharp beak". Instead, she sipped her drink without tasting it and a warm fizz began between her legs as she stared at his sensitive cunt-sucking mouth.

'Let me get you another?' Michael raised his finger and Larry, like magic, placed another cocktail in front of her. 'I just offered to buy you a drink. Nothing more, I didn't want to pick you up and I sure as hell don't care a shit what you're doing here.'

Imogen glanced at his Rolex watch and his fine pair of opal cufflinks and then glanced away; she'd done with being impressed. She'd grown up around affluence and when her mother had made it big she'd seen many fine things. Once a week her mother had taken her to the Ritz and they'd dined in sumptuous luxury eating off small plates with tiny forks while a quartet played in the corner. That was one of the things she had liked about Louis, she had been easily impressed then and Louis had the best of everything. He may have come from the slums in Chicago, but when he made it big in steel he'd indulged himself in every possible way: fine wine and restaurants; clothes and fancy shoes. It didn't take her long, though, to find out that money couldn't buy love.

She supposed she was becoming the perfect facsimile of what her mother had once been. What was it Mama's lover, Herr Cleef, had said about Marianne? It had been like looking at a flawless diamond. Outwardly, it was scintillating and perfect, but examine it closely enough and you saw a glimmer of something fascinatingly dirty. Not the kind of dirt which marred the exterior to any great degree. But, just the slightest trace, rendering the overall effect more exciting. Yes, Mama had possessed classical sophistication, however, despite what she wanted you to believe, she had the innate air of a whore about her in the way she prostituted the legs and the silk stockings and Imogen knew you couldn't shake breeding off. You could pretend to be anything you wanted to be, but class clung to you and when she got down to it, all her mother's good breeding and instruction could not change what she was. You couldn't paint over the small flaw, the black spot of sex which made you behave in a certain way and got you in trouble. Her mother had craved sex and prostituted her legs and got in trouble because of it and now Imogen did the same thing.

For an instant she thought of sex, and she felt herself become juicy and fluid and perhaps a little reckless in how she was thinking. Suddenly, she was craving the touch of a hand and finger, but more than that she craved a voice which said, 'I love you.'

Tomorrow, as soon as she got up, she would go down to the studio and she'd practice her dance exercises in front of the bar and the large mirror and work some of this dangerous energy out of her before she did something stupid. Twice a week she went to a dance class, run to Nazi perfection by Karl, an instructor of the old regime – the regime of sweat and hard work – who made the dance girls struggle so hard to keep limber they were mentally and physically exhausted afterwards. Karl was tough and he looked tough, he had very short blond hair and a face like a crunched up paper bag. The girls said he never spoke to them and if he did he could be gruff and frightening, but he liked Imogen because he could tell she hid a dark secret and the secret made her work harder than most. With his slightly sadistic smile he strolled back and forth shouting his orders, but it was always with a teasing look. 'Come along, Imogen, too much butterkuchen makes you lazy.'

'I'm not trying to pick you up,' Michael said, challenging her with his dark gaze. 'I realise what you're thinking. You think I'm a sleaze bucket and I'm trying to come on to you, but I'm not. I want to talk to you and get beneath that prickly skin of yours.'

'You're too close.' Imogen laughed, pushing him away gently with her hand. 'So close, you're seducing my legs. Do you generally get this personal with a woman you don't know?'

'No,' Michael said shrewdly. 'Of course not. What kind of a man, do you think I am?'

'Well you're a man and that's enough.' She kept rippling her fingers up and down the stem of her glass. 'And you keep staring at me. In particular you insist on staring at my legs? Do you see anything there to interest you?'

'Oh, I can see I'm going to have to be honest. Yes, I do. I never saw such a fabulous pair of legs and I've seen a few in my time. Your legs are pure fantasy but I bet millions of guys tell you that?'

'These legs are certainly not fantasy. They're a very real pair of legs. Jesus, you're just the same as other men, aren't you? Always staring at the legs or the tits. What is it with guys?'

'You prostitute them. That's why,' Michael commented. 'It's hard not to stare when a woman with an outstanding sexual attribute's thrusting it in your face. You must realise you have something there? Some tool of sexual seduction. Hell, it's worse than a bare breast. A pair of silk stockings is far more sexual than a bare breast could ever be.'

Imogen gave a snort of laugher. 'You know that's just what someone else once said to me and he was a bastard.' This was a dangerous conversation so it was convenient that at that precise moment a man entered the bar and Imogen experienced a pulse of alarm. Her whole body stiffened and her lips began to tremble. Today, she speculated, had not been a good day at all and now it was going to be made a whole lot worse by Gunter.

Michael peered first at Imogen and next at the man who he could see had created a flutter around her and a discernible disturbance in the quiet pool of her reflection. Michael watched her lips tighten. She blinked once or twice and then she muttered under her breath, 'Shit, here comes trouble again.'

Gunter was like a missile in the way he homed in on Imogen. He was a large bear of a man with a pock-marked face and a small scar above his top lip. He possessed a savage, twisted expression as if he was extremely angry. Imogen didn't shrink back, but she turned very pale and began fiddling with the clip on her purse. Gunter's arm came out and, grabbing Imogen by the wrist, he tried to pull her off her stool. 'You little whore, Imogen. I've been searching everywhere for you, do you think I have time for this? I guess I should have looked here first. Found the vixen in her lair.'

'You're hurting me,' Imogen said, trying to pull her arm away. But, Gunter had locked on to it like a bull terrier and he was not about to let go.

'I ought to smack you. You cunt broad,' he said, raising his hand to slap her as his eyes flashed maliciously. 'You can't simply walk out like that. I booked you for a private party and you let me down. You made me look a real dickhead.'

'Fuck off,' Imogen retorted tightly. Her heart was pounding and she felt giddy. 'You don't own me. I just agreed to dance for your shitty little party, that's all. But you didn't warn me, huh. You didn't warn me about the arsehole with the wandering hands. The slimeball went and put his hand on my cunt and I'd had enough.'

'What do you expect? You're nothing but a two-bit

whore and you do nothing but provoke.'

Immediately, Michael was on his feet. With one hand he gripped Gunter by the scruff of the neck and with the other he twisted the man's arm up between his shoulder blades. 'Whoa, hold on a minute, buster. Didn't anyone ever tell you? You never raise a hand to a lady.'

'And who do you think you are?' Gunter replied, his lips parting in a watery grin. 'You want me to knock your block off, because I will!'

'You're welcome to try,' Michael said. 'But you'll be hearing from my attorney if you do. Do you know who I am? I'm Michael Levenstein?' Michael rarely pulled rank but he felt a glow of satisfaction as he watched the man fold like a stack of cards.

'Well OK, buster. Perhaps I overreacted a little. But Imogen, she ain't no lady, and the both of us had an agreement. I paid her a small fortune for a private dance after her show.'

Reaching in his wallet, Michael extracted a wad of German marks and he pushed them into Gunter's jacket pocket. 'Here's what she owes you plus a bit of interest on the investment. Now you can go out and buy a more accommodating whore.'

Gunter stared uncertainly at Michael, his eyes roving over him, from the tips of his two tone shoes to the top of his head, and then he shrugged. 'Well, all I can say is good luck, buster. 'Cause you're gonna need it.'

Imogen shivered as she watched Gunter leave the bar, and then, tugging on her jacket, she slithered off the stool and picked her purse up off the counter. When she stood up, she was of average height but her legs were spectacular and disproportionately longer than her body. She was all leg and silk stockings and nothing much else. She was an erotic fantasy.

'Thank you,' Imogen said. 'I could have handled it, though. I have to handle it, since my little whore world is full of nothing but pervy arseholes like him. It's the nature of what I do. I'm a dancer and by now you'd think I'd have learnt a lesson or two about the kind of company I keep, wouldn't you? But that's just it, I don't learn and I can't be fussy.' Raising her skirt she caressed her thigh before letting the fabric drop. 'Silk stockings cost big bucks and what are you staring at?' She placed her hands on her hips and waved her hand dismissively. 'Yeah, yeah. I know what you're going to say. I asked for it, I shouldn't have lowered myself to dance for a slimeball like Gunter. But I'm nothing special and I have to put bread on the table.' And then she stretched out one of her gorgeous legs and moved it this way and that. 'Since I have this, it makes sense to sell it.'

'It strikes me,' Michael commented. 'A woman with your class ought to watch who she's associating with. So, you're not a whore. But you prostitute your art, which is the art of wearing fine silk stockings. I don't know which is worse. A straightforward whore plying her body, or a whore of the silk stocking.'

'But you can afford to be fussy, Mr Michael Levenstein.' She leaned so close to Michael her breath stroked his cheek. 'I know who you are, you big shot. Only last month I saw your big shot attorney papa, in a fancy magazine, hey he's standing for senator isn't he? So, I wonder, do you have a secret too? Why do you work for a cosmetics company when you could be rolling in dough?'

Michael laughed. 'Sure, you got me there.' He was straightening his tie. 'But, it's like this. 'I've got reasons to be doing what I'm doing and I hazard a guess you've got reasons to be doing what you're doing. I'm also not my father.'

'You!' She poked Michael in the breastbone. 'You're an argumentative pig and you think you have a clever way with words. But I like you. So, what the hell, I was lucky to be born with a gift, I have terrific legs and I'm a good dancer. Well.' She drew herself up to her full height placing her hands on her hips. 'In this world it's often not enough just to have a gift. Now, if I was only a little more beautiful or a bit taller. Or, for instance, I'd been born into social advantage, things wouldn't be this way. I'd be touring the world dancing like all the famous dancers or maybe like my mama, I'd be a fashion model and I'd model good hose.' She fluttered her eyelashes as once again she saucily extended a splendid leg. 'But that's another story. Instead, I prostitute the legs as you say and I do it with class and I know how to wear a pair of good silk stockings. Men can't take their eyes off my stockings.' She drew her skirt up higher still, revealing the gorgeous hand made lace seams of her silk hose and a pair of dainty black satin suspenders and with a flick of her fingers she slid a card out of the top of one of her stockings and presented it to Michael with a flourish. 'You see, I really am a dancer. I work for a decent burlesque club in one of the better parts of town.' She did a toe tap on the floor, the silk stockings rippling like the surface of a glassy lake. Before moving her skirt this way and that she performed a number of sexy balletic movements with her leg. 'But, it's no ordinary show.'

Hooking her heel behind Michael's pants leg she ran her foot up the inside of his thigh before rocking back on her heels and laughing. 'I've scandalised you, haven't I? You don't know what to make of me? Now, here's what I think you should do. I think you should come and see me dance. All you have to do is show the card and say you're a friend of Imogen's and they'll sit you in the front row. Then you'll see what a prostitution of the leg's truly about.'

Leaning forward, she brushed his lips with a butterfly kiss, she couldn't resist it. He looked so naïve, so fabulously sexy standing there with his tie askew and his messy blond hair flopping over his eyes. 'Although you don't think I do, I actually appreciate your kindness, Mr Levenstein.'

Imogen's heart had slowed down to a tick tock and she felt pleasantly warm and giddy as she looked into his face.

She wanted to touch him and she did. She wanted to feel that warm male flesh and she wanted to fondle his tight nipples. She'd always liked a man's nipples. Her hands slid under his jacket and caressed his hips. Michael was spellbound.

'I'll see you there, won't I, Mr Levenstein?' And she flashed him a smile. 'You'll come and watch me, won't you?' Then brushing his cheek with her lips, Imogen vanished between the tables.

Chapter Three

WHEN HE GOT BACK to his hotel room Michael would be alarmed to find one of Imogen's silk stockings hanging from the inside pocket of his jacket. He'd take it out and sit and stare at it for a moment, unsure exactly what kind of message the gesture was meant to convey. She'd hidden it when she kissed him, since there was no other way the limp piece of silk could have come to be there. Earlier Imogen had taken off an old laddered hose and taking a new one, which she carried in her purse, she'd changed it. Because she liked Michael and she wanted him to think about her, she'd then cleverly placed the old hose in his pocket. That was one of the things about working in the kind of club she worked in, she rubbed shoulders with a lot of different people and one of them was a two-bit magician who had taught her a useful trick or two about hands in pockets.

Michael would rub the stocking and stretch it across his fingers. Only hours before, the stocking had been fondling and kissing her skin like a glove, massaging her moist intimate places and held in suspense above the throbbing woman part of her. When he held it to his nose it was laced with the odour of sweet cologne and an even sweeter musky feminine scent. The unique sex scent of Imogen. She had done it to deliberately provoke him and she'd succeeded, because she knew what he'd do with the silk stocking. Filled with a wild fetishistic urge, Michael would wrap it around his hand and, stripping out of his clothes, massage his entire naked body and then his dick with it, before folding the silk stocking over his cock and ejaculating into it.

The next day he'd discover he was noticing women and the hose they wore as if it had become an addiction with him. Most women didn't wear their hose in the way Imogen did, though. It was as if Imogen had honed his perception for silk stocking prostitution to perfection and spoilt the seduction possibilities of hose for the majority of the rest of the world's female population.

Chapter Four

THE CLUB WAS DARK and intimate, but unlike many Berlin strip clubs it possessed an element of class and sophistication. On a darkened stage, a procession of burlesque dancers appeared and disappeared from behind a heavy red brocade curtain, each dancer seeming to have a unique themed routine to do with her body or an item of clothing because that was what the Blue Palm Club did, it specialised in unique beauties.

Michael was thrilled by the performances and found he was clapping each girl with evident enjoyment. One girl prostituted her breasts in a number of scintillating costumes and fringed sparkling tassels, while another prostituted her exceptional butt.

When Imogen eventually appeared as the star turn, she was wearing a black tie and tails and she did a routine, which involved the use of a long silver topped cane, a top hat and a straight backed, elegant chair. The tails had been specially tailored to ride up her thighs and a longer than normal vent opened and closed to provide tantalising glances of her miniscule black panties, suspenders and her seamed black silk stockings. Her complicated dance routine was a symphony of erotic improvisation, involving a number of sexy dances around the carefully positioned chair on which Imogen posed to great effect and to much adulation and hand clapping.

She was amazingly dextrous and erotic and as usual she oozed sex. Her legs possessed such elasticity it was impossible not to be mesmerised by her intricate acrobatics, the bending this way and that and the contortion into all sorts of complicated poses. Michael was not to know she despised prostituting her legs and every moment she was on stage she had carefully trained her mind to think of other things. She couldn't see the audience, and good thing too, because the floodlights were angled in such a way all Imogen saw was vacant smoky darkness and that made it easier in a way. Tonight, she strolled around in a haze of hopeful expectation. She didn't know if Michael was there, but she hoped he was.

Positioning her chair, she leant her chin on it and blinked into the lights. One moment her feet were up on the chair and her knees were opening and closing like a pair of scissors, the next they were over the back of the chair and Imogen was leaning backwards with her face turned to Michael and her hand on the floor. Her luscious blonde hair fell in a cascade around her face and the coat fell over her cheeks to reveal the glorious forward thrust of her legs, the sexy suspenders and the panties with just the barest hint of pubic hair.

For the grand finale, she leapt to her feet and paraded around with the silver topped cane, stroking the silk stockings with it and running it up her thighs, and then she did a saucy turn with the cane between her legs while she pouted and sang and fluttered her eyelashes.

After the show, she came down from the stage and finding Michael at the small table she sat on his knee and gently palpated his erection. 'How did you find the show?' she asked boldly.

Grinning, Michael moved his hand over her buttocks and lifting the coat he smoothed his hands along the insides of her silk stockings. Imogen enjoyed the feel of his hands, it was a long time since a man had touched her carefully and she placed her hand on his cheek. When he looked at her she realised it wasn't simply an addiction for the silk stockings. He had that far away look which told her he was a guy falling in love with the silk stocking whore.

'I swear I never met a girl like you, Imogen. You're crazy.'

She clasped her hands around his neck. 'Do you think so? OK, I'm crazy and a whore of the silk stockings?' Instantly, her gaze froze and she began nibbling at her bottom lip. 'There's so much you don't know about me, Michael – like Gunter, for instance. He followed me for a while when I left the bar last night and it freaked me out. He was hanging about here all day too, wearing his thunderous expression. He's a bad man, Michael. I seem to have this penchant for attracting rotten men into my life. Do you think it'd be a bad thing if I asked you to walk me home tonight, since I feel …?' She wriggled her buttocks against Michael's erection. 'I feel a teensy bit scared for some reason.'

'No, of course not,' Michael said, caressing the silk stockings with small palm movements of his hand. 'I'd be delighted to.'

'Thank you, it's very kind of you, it's quite a way.'

She was scared, that much was true, but not for the reasons she'd given. It was not Gunter who scared her half to death – he was all bluster but harmless – no, it was someone else. For three nights now when Imogen put on her coat and came out of the club, she was sure she'd seen a shadow clinging to the buildings and that shadow made her skin crawl. She could be imagining it, of course. If you lived with fear for a great many years you could imagine all sorts of things.

In order to get to her apartment, she had to walk to the tram stop and take the tram quite a distance before getting off. Then, it was a walk along a few dark and not very well lit streets into a shabby part of Berlin, peppered with community housing. She shivered when she thought of it, however, it was necessary because a better apartment would cost a great deal of money and the very intricacy of the streets gave her anonymity.

She sucked her lip, she had an awfully bad feeling. It had crept up on her like a dark cloud and had started two months ago with the call from her old friend, Martha Braun. Imogen had told Martha never to call her on the phone in the lobby because she felt too vulnerable standing there, but Martha said she'd had to break the golden rule because there was something she ought to know. Imogen had become frozen, her hands and feet like blocks of ice. Louis was out of prison.

Imogen always slid in and out of the apartment like a wraith, she was so paranoid about it, now she was more scared than ever. When you had something valuable in your life and you wanted to protect it, that was how you became. She preferred to go out after dark, but when she was forced to leave during the day she pulled the collar of her coat up, scraped her hair back into a coil down her back and she wore no make-up.

She sat back coquettishly, swinging her legs back and forth and drawing little spirals on the back of his hand. 'Did you find my little present, Michael? It was a bad thing for me to do, but I can be impetuous. I try to be good, I really do, but there's a part of me which is very bad indeed.'

'And what present would that be?' Michael replied. He seemed determined to play her at her own game.

'Naughty. You know exactly what present.' Her gaze travelled over his face. His eyes were wide and glistening and there was a hungry look about them. Imogen couldn't tell him, she'd thought about him last night. For the first time it wasn't Anni who'd claimed her thoughts, but Michael. She could almost feel the curve of his body, the way he held her and she pushed back against him and felt his erection pushing between her legs. Imogen took his earlobe between her neat square teeth and bit it gently. 'Don't fool with me, Michael. You found the silk stocking, didn't you? I knew you were craving one. I could tell by the hungry look in your eyes. Every man wants to touch and play with my silk stockings and they all want to have one. For a moment there I became silly and a bit childish and I thought, I like Mr Michael Levenstein immensely and I want to thank him. What can I give him as a thank you present? So I made you a gift of the silk stocking. And after I did it, I lay in bed all night imagining what you were doing and if you were titillating your dick with it. Did you do that? You see I have fantasies too.'

Michael took Imogen's hand and then he turned it over and kissed her palm, circling it with his tongue as Imogen's eyes glowed with pleasure.

'I might have thought about it a little bit, but it would have been bad of me having thoughts of that nature about a nice girl like you.'

'Nice girl! Oh, I wish you knew about me and then you'd change your mind.'

'I want to find out about you, if you'd let me.' He jiggled her on his lap. 'I'd like to take you out to this fabulous little café where they have the best hot chocolate in Berlin.'

Imogen licked her lips, she loved chocolate and she felt an orgasmic frisson at the thought of it. She was on a very strict budget and she rarely stopped at cafés since she was carefully saving every penny for Anni and putting it into a savings account. It meant there was nothing left over for any treats.

'I don't know.'

Michael was frowning. 'I asked Larry about you. I didn't want to tread on any guy's toes if you were dating. He said you didn't seem to have a guy, so, I got to thinking.'

'What, you thought I was maybe a lesbian?'

'No, I didn't think that, not in the least.' Michael slipped his arm around her waist and caressed her gently with his thumb. 'I thought perhaps here's a woman who's been stung by love. A beautiful single woman with haunted eyes.'

Imogen was afraid because Michael was staring at her with the same intensity Louis had stared at her, except it lacked the fierceness. Louis had been frightening in his obsessive love for her.

'Is it possible you're falling a little bit in love with me, Michael? You are, aren't you? But, you don't have to admit it if you don't want to. After all you are the great Michael Levenstein and I guess you can have any woman in the world you want.' She paused. 'I'd have to say to you if you were considering falling in love with me, it's a very bad idea.'

'Why?' Michael asked.

Imogen shrugged. 'No man would want to become involved with me, because I'm complicated and I attract trouble.'

Michael shrugged. 'I can take a bit of trouble and you're right, women throw themselves at me all the time.'

Imogen stared at him, she didn't know if he was kidding or not.

'However, maybe I don't want any woman in the world.' Michael stroked a loose tendril of hair out of her eye. 'Perhaps I want a silk stocking whore.'

'You're not lying, are you?'

'Sadly no,' Michael replied.

'We're playing a little game aren't we, Michael, and it feels nice but it's such a long time ago that I was in love? I don't know if it would be such a good thing to have a romance with an American.'

Michael took her hand, turning it over and then he kissed it and ripples of pleasure welled up in Imogen and the place between her legs opened and became wet and she moved her legs. He pressed his mouth to her palm and she felt his tongue lapping; it was perversely erotic.

'Can't you just take this interlude?' he said. 'And not make a big thing of it. We like each other, don't we? There was some sort of mutual attraction when we met. Shouldn't we get to know one another because if we didn't, possibly we'd regret it?

Imogen looked at him sadly. She was suffering a battle inside, yet her one overriding desire in that moment was love and how it felt to be loved and absorbed and lose herself in passion. She threaded her fingers through his soft corn coloured hair and planted a kiss on top of his head. The heat which had started in her cheeks seemed to be slowly dribbling in a warm river down her body, ebbing and flowing into her cracks and curves and setting her alight with delicious anticipation.

'Don't you think such legs and such silk stockings need to be worshipped, Michael. Tell me how you'd do that?' Imogen felt very naughty indeed. She knew it was dangerous to tempt and lure, but she couldn't help it. Her eyes were shining and her cheeks were flushed. 'Come along, if you whisper it, no one will hear. Whisper it here in my ear.'

'I think I ought to walk you home right now, before I do something I shouldn't,' Michael said. 'Hop up.'

Giggling, Imogen jumped off his lap and ran to the dressing room, returning a while later dressed in a neat wool suit and carrying the hat and tails over her arm. Michael was waiting for her by the door. He took her hand and held it tightly. As they walked, Imogen's thighs in the silk stockings brushed together with a sound like static and she could see him smiling as he listened to the crackle, crackle of the silk stocking friction. After a while he pulled her closer and whispered in her ear. 'Imogen, what is that way you have of walking with the friction of the stockings rubbing together. Such a thing could ignite a man in flames?'

Imogen gripped his hand and she held it to her thigh and as they strolled along she pressed his fingers to the edge of her lacy seams and he moved his finger beneath her suspenders. 'Either one of us could be set on fire.' She laughed. 'But, perhaps it'll be me and not you.'

On the tram he kept watching her and it made her tingle

all over. Somehow he had found a way to slip beneath her defences. Sometimes she caught him watching her out of the corner of his eye and at other times he watched her reflection in the glass. Michael, she deduced, was like a watery sun popping out from behind a cloud and gently warming her frozen body.

A cold wind blew down the *strasse* and Imogen buttoned her coat as they walked together in silence. She was afraid. Her number one rule when she'd moved here was never to bring men back to the apartment. She had to avoid the possibility of Louis finding out where she lived and worked and to do that she had to learn to keep secrets and lead a solitary life. She'd even made sure she didn't shop at the same shops, just in case she was followed, and her dentist and doctor were right the other side of town.

Her apartment was situated up a narrow side street and reached through a curved archway which led into a courtyard. Searching in her pocket for her key, Imogen unlocked a door into a small shabby halfway and Michael, consumed with excitement, pressed his hands to her thighs and forced her up against the wall. Imogen sighed and shivered as his hands felt under her skirt and stroked between her thighs, then giggling she took his hand and pulled him over to a small elevator. 'It's a curious old building, isn't it? They tell me this section was once part of the old hospital.' She punched a button and the door opened and then slammed with a clang, the two of them ascending in the dark cage which creaked and groaned and occasionally shuddered, like a woman approaching orgasm. Michael held her tightly, with his arm around her waist and his mouth buried in her perfumed hair, and Imogen wondered how it would feel to have his hand right down against her flesh, inside the silk stockings.

The door clattered open and, laughing, Imogen lifted her skirt coquettishly and sashayed along the corridor doing a little dance and walking on the tips of her toes.

'Well this is my little boudoir, Michael,' she said as she leant seductively against the door. 'You must promise you won't be alarmed when you come inside, but I'm rather an untidy girl, I'm afraid. And, since I hardly ever ask men back to my room I don't bother tidying up much. Actually, I can't remember when I last had a real boyfriend, although naturally many men hang around the stage door.'

'Yes I imagine they would,' Michael said huskily.

The apartment was little more than a room situated high up in the attic. However, it had a startling panoramic view of Berlin and, far away, the roof of the cathedral. Through the draughty old window, around which she had stuck pieces of newspaper, the wind whistled with a strange high musical cadence. Imogen watched Michael carefully. She supposed Mr Levenstein lived in a chic loft apartment in the city and was used to opulent surroundings. After all, the Levensteins apparently owned a huge house in the Hamptons, with tennis courts and swimming pools. She'd read about Mr Levenstein senior, he had defended politicians and actors. His wife, Norma, had apparently alienated her children with her overbearing manner but she recalled her own mother had admired the woman – her dresses and shoes, beautiful grooming and impeccable style. Imogen twisted a strand of her hair around her finger. She found it odd and unsettling and like a mysterious twist of destiny, that *the* Michael Levenstein was standing in her little room and that he had a connection, however loosely, with her past and her mother.

'It's not much. But, it's convenient for work. Plus there's the added advantage of Herr Eichel, who owns the bakers and who saves me the leftovers. Herr Eichel makes the most wonderful butterkuchen. I have a small piece left if you'd like it?'

'I can think of another butterkuchen I'd rather have,' Michael murmured.

Imogen flicked on a lamp. 'You can see I'm telling the truth and I don't have many visitors, can't you? It's simply a place to sleep, that's all. Make yourself at home, Michael.'

Imogen began clearing a chair. Taking the strewn clothing she dumped it onto the floor in an untidy pile before carefully placing her top hat and coat onto an old dressmaker's mannequin in the corner of the room.

The room was very shabby indeed with faded flock wallpaper. It was dominated by a Chinese screen in one corner, a huge ornate wardrobe and a French cheval mirror. Nearly every piece of furniture was covered in items of clothing and in particular loose silk stockings, which hung here and there like discarded condoms.

Michael sat down cautiously on the bed, which was covered in a blood red quilt and various items of alluring underwear: real French lace panties and a thin silk chemise. She could tell he was suffering from compelling sexual urges as he kept crossing his legs and tugging his jacked down over his erection, men were so bad at hiding these things.

Imogen was feeling relaxed. She shook a cigarette out of a box on her dressing table and striking a match and cupping the flame, her face was briefly illuminated. Then, smiling, she stubbed it out. She must be excited to so quickly forget one of her promises. Boldly unbuttoning her overcoat, she shrugged it from her shoulders before unfastening her blouse and unzipping her skirt and kicking it away with her foot.

Imogen was now completely naked except for her suspender belt and stockings and her impossibly tall high heels. Next, hooking her leg around the chair she drew it out and sat down at the dressing table. What was it her mother had said? "It was better to be hung as a sheep than a lamb." Michael watched her apply make-up remover to some cotton wool and remove her make-up. Then she pushed open the door of a tiny closet and drawing some water she washed her face and hands and between her legs with a washcloth.

'You don't know what to make of me, do you, Michael?' she said as she strolled back into the room. 'And, it's probably just as well because you'd hate me.'

Michael was staring at Imogen's legs. In the glow from the lamp her stockings shone. She saw him staring, sat down and pushing the chair away a little from the dressing table and knowing she was being deliberately provocative, she crossed her legs extremely slowly, compelling the black suspenders to tighten and pull on the fine inflexible silk. A darkness seemed to be trickling out of her, a desire to be very bad. Louis had made her behave badly, she thought ruefully, but those times had gone. However, sex was such a compulsive human drive, once you had a taste for it, it kept coming back and you couldn't push the itch to be naughty away.

She sat back in the chair, parting her legs and running her hands up the insides of her thighs in a gesture of downright sexual decadence, before trailing her fingers over the curve of her belly and thrusting her hips forward so Michael could see the plush mound of pubic hair between her legs.

'Is that what you mean by butterkuchen? Well, I think you're playing around,' he said. He got to his feet and taking a robe off the back of a mirror he threw it into her lap. 'Cover yourself up or I'll leave this instant.'

Imogen giggled nervously. Frankly, she didn't know what she wanted. She felt scared and confused. She wanted love so desperately she'd do anything for it and yet she was so petrified she dare not risk it, and then there was the other aspect of it. The fact she genuinely liked Michael but she knew if she got to know him in anything but a superficial sense, she'd have to start explaining, and explaining could be so difficult when she didn't know where to start.

'The last time I saw such erotic behaviour was with this broad called Rocella. She was my girlfriend for a while when I was in Brazil and she liked to pose whenever she could in the nude.' Michael strolled back to the bed with his hands in his pockets. 'She oozed sex. She'd pose on chairs and on the edge of her bathtub where she'd sit combing her long wet hair and smoothing it between her breasts. She even stripped off and posed nude on the back seat of my Sedan. Until you, I thought she was the sexiest woman I'd ever encountered. However, to my mind there's nothing more erotic than a woman semi-clad in silk stockings.'

'And what happened to this whore?' Imogen asked, leaning forward and sliding her arms into the sleeves of the robe.

'She wasn't marriage material and she didn't tell me she had a boyfriend who was a drug baron.'

'Ah, I see.' Imogen got up and plucked a photograph from out of a crack in the dressing table mirror. She held it out. 'This is my mother, Michael. Everyone thought she was exceedingly beautiful and very sexy. My mother was German but she went to live in Paris just before the war. She worked for Cervin. You must have heard of Cervin? They make the finest silk stockings in the world. It was heaven for mother, a dream come true. You see, she had incredible legs and she also had this great love of silk stockings. It's a curse this thing the Heinemann women have with the legs and the stockings. Anyway, she'd do anything for a pair of fine silk stockings and didn't consider herself dressed without them.'

Imogen held out the photograph. 'Here take it and have a good look. Doesn't she look lovely? Very sophisticated and quite the lady. Mother was so poor, you know, but she always made the best of herself and wore the best hose money could buy. She said it was essential a woman complete her dress with a pair of fine silk stockings as that was the only way she would seduce and marry a rich man. Mother was of the philosophy that stockings made a woman a true lady but at the same time a whore ... and men love a lady with such a dual personality. It's a man's wet dream to have a lady on his arm to show to his friends and a whore in the bedroom. Well, one day she was coming out of the factory and she caught the eye of this man. A rich industrialist. The man fell in love with the whore of

37

stockings and he used to follow her. At first it scared Mother a little bit so she tried to confound him. She'd walk much further than she needed to. Taking circuitous routes and staying on the metro and going to stops she didn't really want, to try and give him the slip. But he loved her and I'm led to believe it's impossible to shake off a man once he loves you.' Imogen glanced at Michael and saw he was in raptures over the story. 'The trouble is, having never been in love like that, how would I know whether that's true or not? The man pushed her into a doorway and tried to seduce her. His hands were all over her fine silk stockings and he kept saying. I'm in love with you, Marianne. Give me a stocking as a memento and I'll leave my wife.'

Imogen took a loose stocking off her dressing table and holding it like a scarf she used it as a screen, stretching it tightly across her mouth. 'I think all the Heinemann women from the dawn of time must have been silk stocking coquettes, because my mother unclipped and unrolled her stocking right there in the street and rubbing it in her cunt and pushing it inside her vagina which was so wet for this man who she fancied like hell … she held it out and she said, "Here's a gift for you." The man laughed and he said, "You're adorable, you whore. I love you." Then he smelt the stocking and he said, "There's no smell like your cunt. I could find your cunt in the whole of Paris from this stocking." He got mother a job modelling for a fashion house and she was good at it, she was taller than me, she was made to wear good clothes not just Cervin.'

'I don't believe that,' Michael said.

'You can believe what you choose, Michael. Well it was inevitable she'd fall in love since my mother was such a romantic woman. All the Heinemanns are senseless in love. But it was complicated you know, love's always so complicated.'

Imogen retrieved the picture and, kissing her finger and placing it on her mother's face, she placed the photograph back in the frame of the mirror. 'Mother had an affair with the man, it lasted nearly ten years. She was very much in love and as a result here I am. Yes, Michael, I'm a chip off the old block since I'm the bastard daughter of – how should we say? – the prostitute of the leg or the woman in the silk stockings. That's why I'm a crazy broad.'

'What happened?' Michael asked.

'He left her stranded when she got pregnant, as most married men do. Mama had a great deal of money by then but she was so sad, she just spent it, spent it on good things to make her forget. You know – nice clothes for me, tea at the Ritz. Money is like water through a bucket though, and soon spilt.'

'What a sad story,' Michael said.

'It wasn't easy for my mother.' She smiled at him in the mirror. 'I hate sad stories don't you?'

'Yes,' he said. 'I only deal in happy endings and what about you, have you ever been in love?'

Imogen's heart was fluttering. 'Good question. Frankly, I don't know. Once I thought I was, but now I'm not so sure. Love is so many things.'

'I only deal in true love, passionate one and only love. Like I only deal in those happy endings.' Michael grinned.

Imogen bit her lip because she was inclined to believe him, there was something about the great Michael Levenstein.

'You see.' She held up the silk stocking, waving it back and forth like a used condom. 'These are the only kind I wear. The first time I wore silk stockings was when I was six. I looked funny. I stole mother's stockings and I pulled them on. They were much too long for me, though, and kept falling off. I must have made such a comical picture. And, they'll also be the last thing I wear, Michael. Because I want to be buried in a casket wearing the most expensive silk stockings money can buy. Don't you think I'm a bit of a caution? Aren't I a little bit too hot to handle?'

Imogen couldn't tear her gaze away as she stared at him in the mirror and then she began to unpin her long blonde hair shaking it out and brushing it with long strokes of her hairbrush. A disturbing idea had come into her head, a "what if?" idea. What if I fucked Michael? Who would know and it's cold and coming winter and I need the warmth and it could feel so good to fuck and then have a man, a nice man like Michael to twist and curl around – and if I asked him to leave before it got light so no one saw, I'm sure it would be all right. Taking a deep breath, she said, 'I'm giving you one last chance to go before, well … you know.'

'What kind of an *opt out* clause?' Michael enquired, staring at her breasts which gave her a weird shiver.

'Yes, in legal terms I guess that's it. Do you always think in legal terms?'

She came and sat beside him and he took her hand and twining his fingers through hers he held them to her mouth in an oddly old-fashioned gesture. 'Sure.' He was thoughtful. 'But, when I came up here I knew I wouldn't leave.'

'This is a fuck, right?' Imogen said quietly, as she studied the sensitive bow of his mouth and leaning forward kissed him lightly. 'And that's all it is? It'd be stupid in view of all the dark things in my life, to think that it could go further. And, what are you – a travelling salesman? And isn't that what travelling salesmen do? Fuck and move on?'

Michael shrugged as she undid one of his buttons and touched the throbbing pulse at his throat.

'Perhaps, I have secrets of my own and my life isn't what you think.'

'What, you're a communist spy or something? Come on,' Imogen coaxed.

'I might be.' He paused and his breath was warm and sweet on her hand. 'Would it excite you if you thought I was a spy?'

'No, I don't think it would, I've had enough intrigue in

my life.'

Michael kissed her and each of her fingers.

'So,' she said eventually. 'What kind of a fantasy do you have? Is it of the general kind? For instance, how would you like it if I took a pair of my fine silk stockings and I tied you hand and foot to the bed?' Strolling to her chest of drawers she tugged it open and out spilled a profusion of stockings. 'Once I saw a woman struggling into a pair of cheap stockings in a public toilet. She took them out of her shopping bag. They were so vulgar it made me feel sick. I could never wear those ghastly things. No, for me it must be the best and as a result, I'll always be poor. Here, handle these and you'll see what I mean.'

Imogen took a packet and slowly she began extracting the silk stockings, rubbing them across her nose and mouth before handing one to Michael. 'These are the finest stockings money can buy. They're the Cervin. You see, they're so fine. Only one denier and so incredibly thin they're like a second skin. A pair of these stockings is really expensive and you can only buy them in the most exclusive boutiques. When I go into a shop and I buy a pair of these, it's such a treat I feel like a queen. You see why I have to do stupid things such as private shows for perverts like Gunter, and the dance classes at the seedy little club. It's so I can have life's simple silk pleasures. I can tell you Cervin gives me a better orgasm than any man.'

She sat back down on the bed beside Michael. 'You can move my stuff, you know. You're still sitting on my panties and you're wriggling like a worm. Poor Michael!' Taking the silk stocking from his fingers and smiling she stretched it across his mouth. 'So you have a little thing for the silk stockings.'

'Not just any silk stockings. Your silk stockings, Imogen.'

She forced him back on the bed. 'There, lie down.' And she began trailing the silk stocking over his face. 'I think

41

this is how my mother must have felt.' Imogen placed her hand on her breast and moved it around. 'Oh yes. I think her heart was going pitter-patter, pitter-patter and that was the moment she knew she was in love. You're a handsome man, Mr Levenstein. But you know that, don't you? I only read the short article in the magazine, so I hardly know anything about you. Do you keep a low profile in your private life? Are you married? I expect like mother's lover, you'll turn out to be married.'

'No, I'm not married.' His green eyes fixed on hers, travelled over her face, it was more than lust and the thought of what could be terrified her.

Imogen's fingers were loosening his other shirt buttons one by one. 'There, I think you'll feel a little bit more relaxed if I loosen you up. You're a little uptight and shy but I enjoy that and everything you think shows in your eyes as well. You have expressive eyes, Mr Levenstein.' And she continued to trail the stocking across his face as, lying extremely close to Michael, she pressed her thigh to his leg and her breasts against his shirt, which she was finishing unbuttoning and stripping away from his body. Each time she moved he could hear the thrilling crackle of silk as she rubbed her legs up and down his pants.

'So, if you don't want to be tied to the bed with my silk stockings. What do you want?' Perhaps you'd like to tie me to the bed with them instead. Or ...' Placing her mouth on his she began kissing him with rapier sharp kisses. '... Perhaps you'd like me to play with the silk stockings like this? Watch, Michael.' And, stretching the stockings between her fingers, she straddled him on the bed and with her tongue balancing provocatively on the edge of her lips, she took a fine pair of the Cervin, tying one silk stocking around the groin of her left leg and one around the right before pressing one of the limp pieces of silk to Michael's lips.

Michael kissed the stocking and ran his tongue all over it

until it was wet.

Next, Imogen stretched behind her and fastening the end of the stocking to her suspender belt she tugged it forward through her sex slit and fastened it with a loop at the front.

Michael was speechless and holding his breath. Static surges of lust were pulsing through his system as he fought the uncontrollable urge to roll her on to her back and plunge his swollen cock straight into her.

Imogen wriggled forward until her ripe spilt peach was resting by his mouth.

'You made me a chastity belt?' he whispered.

'Yes,' Imogen replied. 'And tomorrow I won't wear my panties to work. I'll wear nothing but this chastity belt, beneath my clothes.'

Michael stared into her face as he trailed his finger across her cheeks. 'You're extraordinary,' he said. 'You fascinate me and I think I love you.'

'Are you sure about that, baby? Are you sure you're not in love with my silk stockings?'

'Yes, naturally I adore your silk stockings, but I also love everything about you. Say! Why don't you marry me and I could buy you a wardrobe of Cervin?'

'You're a funny guy,' Imogen shrieked. 'I don't know whether to take you seriously or not.' And with two or three deft jerks she ripped the recalcitrant zipper down over his erection and pulling down his pants, Imogen gave a sigh as she sat staring at his tumescent erection. After several seconds of studious contemplation she leapt on the bed and lying back on the pillows with her arms above her head she dragged her fingers through her abundant hair.

'There now you can finger my silk stockings.'

'First of all, I'd like you to take them off,' Michael said. 'And next I want you to put them back on again, very slowly.'

'Oh, that's easily done,' Imogen said, sitting up and unclipping one of the stockings from her suspender belt and rolling it down her leg. 'There, is that how you like it? Did you realise there's great skill to putting on and taking off a pair of silk stockings? Shall I show you Michael?'

Removing the silk stocking completely, she threw it on the bed before unrolling the other one. Michael took each one and held it to his nose, then he stroked the pale flesh of Imogen's leg right up to her crotch and the pouting peachy flesh and back down again.

'You don't just pull on a silk stocking,' Imogen continued, wriggling to the edge of the bed and then getting to her feet to fetch another packet of the Cervin. 'It's an art and you have to do it like this. Many years ago, I did a striptease in a small bar in Marseille. I was so good at taking the stockings on and off I drove all the guys crazy.'

Tearing the packet open, she held the stockings to her nose. 'I simply adore the smell of new silk stockings.' And then, with her gaze firmly fixed on Michael, she opened the stocking suggestively before easing her hand inside and placing her foot on the bed. 'Look how fine this is. You could put your finger through it really easily. That's why I keep my nails this short ... and when you hold it up to your eyes you can see straight through it.' Imogen held the hose up to her face creating a veil.

Michael's erection surged forward painfully and he covered the thrusting tumescence with his hand. Through the fine silk, Imogen was blinking and fluttering her eyelashes at him. It was like watching a beautiful woman through the frosted lens of a camera.

'Pay attention.' Raising her foot and balancing on one leg she flexed her toes and wriggling them, she eased the stocking over her foot and up her heel before unrolling it over her leg and drawing it up her thigh, and all to the delicious accompaniment of the hiss of fine silk.

'It's necessary to flex the leg and adjust the silk exceedingly carefully. There's no nylon in these stockings, you see, and absolutely no give.' Her tongue was balancing on her lip in concentration. 'You must be careful you don't tear them. You slide the stocking up the thigh, not too slowly and not too fast. Smoothing it on, just so.' With a deft flick of her finger she attached the stocking to the suspender belt. Then she moved her leg this way and that. 'You must agree the wearing of a silk stocking is an art?'

'Yes I agree. Now, darling Imogen. Let me put on the other one.'

'But you will be careful, won't you?. You'll do it carefully so you don't tear it?'

Before she could move out of the way Michael had tumbled Imogen onto the bed, pulling her full lips down onto his and kissing her while Imogen, giggling and trembling with excitement, beat him gently with the other silk stocking. 'You promise, don't you, Michael.'

'I promise,' he said, gripping a handful of her hair and holding her head still. 'Imogen you're really something, do you know that? I love you. Marry me. I'm not kidding. I'd buy out Cervin for you. Your wardrobe could be full of silk stockings.'

'Aha! A hostile takeover. So, you think you can buy me with silk stockings, huh?' And as Michael squeezed her breasts and nibbled on her nipples, Imogen's hand reached down and making a noose and twisting the silk stocking around and around his swollen dick, she pulled harder and harder whilst her hand alternately played up and down his shaft and her agile fingers tightened the diaphanous silk.

Then flopping back on the bed with her hair loose around her shoulders, she raised her leg, and Michael placed his hand in one of the discarded stockings and began unrolling it on to her foot. He kissed each square inch of flesh before proceeding to the next. Eventually, with shaking fingers, he attached the stocking to the suspender and pressing his hand between the stocking clad thighs, he buried his mouth in her thatch and pulling aside the wet silk chastity belt he tongued her to a gently crooning orgasm.

45

'I can't wait,' Michael said kissing her and feeling the roll of her hips beneath his. 'Untie the stocking from my dick and let me fuck you.'

Imogen giggled. 'My, my. Perhaps I will but only if you agree to let your stick wear my silk stocking.'

Speechless, Michael watched her take his swollen shaft and straddling his hips she unwound the stocking and pinning his arms above his head she stared into his eyes.

'I bet you never wore a condom silk stocking, Michael.' She glanced at him contemplatively and blew gently over his face before outlining each of his eyes and his lower lip with her finger. 'You have nice lips. They're very sensual.' She kissed him gently and Michael's body seemed to liquefy as he watched her, spellbound.

'And, this is my little fantasy,' she said, winking at him as her delicate pink tongue darted out and caressed his cock. Imogen stretched open the stocking and began rolling it over her hand. Next, she smeared the nectar droplets from his weeping cock on her breasts before she tugged the silk stocking down along the head of his penis.

'There you see. I knew all along you were a whore, a silk stocking whore,' Michael said. 'How else would you know how to make a silk condom out of a silk stocking?'

Imogen massaged the sensitive skin of his cockhead before folding the silk stocking over and over, she twisted the fragment of material over Michael's turgid shaft and balls. Then, seizing his ramrod hard dick and pulling aside the silk stocking of the chastity belt, she lowered herself with agonising slowness onto the silk stocking condom. God, it felt so good she could scream and she almost did. The only way she could stop herself was to bite her tongue and clench her teeth.

'You have to admit, the silk stocking gives great friction. Did you ever feel such a fabulous condom, Michael?' She moaned, as she bounced gently up and down and Michael's penis slithered into the tight constriction of silk stocking heaven. No sex for so long had made her needy and her cunt, indeed all of her, cried out for it. In that instant the powerful narcotic which was sex made her forget everything, it made her forget the danger, and the strict rules she'd set herself and it even made her forget Louis. Michael was gentle and soft and he was careful. He allowed her to take the lead, he enjoyed a woman's dominant sex, but more importantly she could tell he understood women and how their minds worked. Momentarily, she felt a piercing pain, an aching tenderness. She was aching as much for him as herself, because tomorrow when she said *no* - which she knew she'd have to - it would feel as powerfully intense as the petit mort which would soon send her into a rapture.

Michael grabbed Imogen's neat little hips and sliding his hand beneath the wet silk, he tugged on the chastity stocking and fucked the silk stocking whore, while she cried out and beat his chest with her fists.

She didn't have an orgasm because it was too fresh and new and the shuddering pulses were like small snarl ups of traffic on the boulevard; things rushed forward too quickly for a moment – her emotions knotting up – then came to a grinding halt. It was continual stop and start, the smooth climb would come later. For now the surges of intense pleasure were enough.

Michael bound her wrists and ankles with Cervin and he gently massaged her all over with the wet condom sheath of the silk stocking. This was good, she thought, as she lay with her arms above her head watching him. It was endearing how much like a child he was, exploring something he'd never had, but probably dreamed about. The fantasy was giving him pleasure; she could tell that from his ramrod hard cock which kept weeping moisture from the tip and which she ached to take in her mouth.

Then Michael lay down beside her and kissed her. 'You didn't say you'd marry me?' he said sadly. 'I think you'd be crazy not to. However, until you agree, I'll hold you captive.'

'There's just one thing,' she said, as she rubbed her legs together and he heard the hiss of the silk stockings. 'I still have one last fantasy.'

'And what's that.' Michael smiled.

'In my fantasy, from the day I get married, my husband becomes the one who always dresses me and puts on my silk stockings. Every day he buys me Cervin. He takes the silk stockings out of the packet and he says, "darling, it's necessary I do this one thing for you".' She pouted coyly. 'It's a lot to ask a man to be a slave of the silk stocking and I'm not sure many would agree to it. But, those are the terms of the agreement.'

Michael untied the stockings so he could hold her and Imogen could place her arms around his neck and stroke her fingers through his hair. 'My darling,' he whispered. 'I think that could easily be arranged.' He then eased his finger beneath the saturated silk stocking and rubbed it back and forth over her agitated slit. It burnt with a satisfying heat like fire and she felt the throb of orgasm return. Next, gathering her up in his arms, he kissed her lips and trailed his fingers down the length of her spine. She couldn't help it, her hand came around his cock and she squeezed it gently and taking some of his juice she smeared it over her lips. She really was behaving like a whore.

Michael kissed her again and his hard cock pushed between her legs. She slithered down the bed and she began licking his balls and Michael vibrated like a piano wire. He was curious in love. He curled into a foetal ball and as she fucked him with her mouth, lips and tongue, he stroked her hair and massaged her scalp, fast and slow, soft and hard and she worked her mouth accordingly, sliding her tongue up the underside of his rod to the tip and then seducing it with kisses before taking it in and biting it, running her tongue around it and sucking it.

'God, I'm sorry.' Michael shuddered and sighed and for a

moment his hands were still. He tugged her hair and she came back up the bed and he stared into her eyes. 'Roll over, honey.' He obviously didn't lose interest after orgasm like most men did. Imogen rolled over and he worked her slowly and for a long time, pinching and stroking her nipples, as he held her snuggled back up against him with his hands caressing her breasts. She ached between her legs for satisfaction as the stocking cut into her cunt and with her finger she wriggled it aside and slid her finger up her slit to relieve herself. He brushed aside her hand and put his there instead and he did it for her. He was very good, she thought, as she came, pushing out her hips against his hand.

Imogen set her alarm for four o'clock. Then she watched him sleep for a while and she gently kissed his cheeks and lips. The warm surge of love was painful but she had to cauterise it. Sitting up, she frowned into the mirror. She knew what she had to do and it was better not to think about it. She gathered up his clothes and began folding them and putting them on the chair and then she opened his wallet. Inside the wallet he had a card and on it he had his address – a fancy address in Manhattan – just as she'd thought, and there was a small picture of a woman she supposed was his mother. She peered out with steel grey eyes from a posed photograph; she looked like a WASP, a socialite. Imogen had a hatred of such women, but her eyes were soft and kind. She pressed her mouth to Michael's shirt to smell his cologne and put it down. When she turned around he was awake and watching her.

'This is my alarm call, is it?'

'Yes, Michael I'm afraid so.'

He stretched and sat naked on the side of the bed. He had a fine body. It was perhaps a little too slim but it was as she liked her lovers, muscular and covered with a scattering of fine blond body hair. He was erect again, however, so, she tried to ignore it.

'You've still got it on.' He laughed.

'What the chastity belt? Oh yes, I told you I wouldn't take it off, didn't I?'

He stood up and coming to her he grabbed her and holding her close he kissed her neck and cheeks. 'When can I see you then?'

'I told you earlier, when we were making love, it's impossible. We can't see each other again, this was, how do they say? A one off.'

Michael was frowning. 'But why? I don't see it. You're single, aren't you?'

She stared at him and her eyes were dark. 'This is just what I didn't want, that's why involvement's better avoided.'

Michael dressed. She could tell he was angry by the way he pulled on his clothes. When he'd finished and was combing his hands through his hair he took a pen and he wrote something on a piece of paper. 'This is the address of the place where I'm staying.'

'Michael I told you there's no point.'

'Yes, there is. Because I don't believe you can hold out.' He touched her cheek. 'I love you.'

She followed him to the door naked, aware as she did so that she looked absurd. 'How can you say that when you only fucked me once?'

'I knew when I first laid eyes on you.' And reaching down he put his finger through the chastity belt and drawing her close he stuck his finger in her cunt. 'Besides, you got the nature of the game wrong. This is the thing about any kind of mental bondage; the guy has the key to the device.' He bent down and as he feathered his tongue in her ear he wrapped the silk stocking chastity belt around his finger, drawing it deeper into her crotch. 'I got the keys to this and remember you said you wouldn't take it off.'

Imogen was experiencing a weird churning, it was half excitement and half fear; she wet her lips as she opened the door.

'You haven't seen the last of me,' Michael said as she closed it.

Chapter Five

IMOGEN WAS AFRAID AND Adele Weinberger only added to her nervousness by knocking on her door that morning to say she'd seen a man on the corner of the street. Imogen leant against the door with her lips pinched and her arms crossed defensively. 'Are you absolutely sure?'

'I saw him once or twice before.' Adele nodded her steel grey head.

'And what was he like?'

'I think it's him, Imogen, he was a broad man built like a wrestler and he had a dark coat and a hat, just like you said.'

'Did you see his face?'

Adele paused. 'Yes. He had a mean face with one lip twisted up, like he had a permanent grimace or something.'

Imogen sagged against the door. There was nothing for it, when Adele left she tidied up the flat and she put all her clothes into her old suitcase and took the steamer trunk off the top of her wardrobe. Then she went downstairs to the telephone in the hall and she called Helga Streiber to say she wouldn't be along to see Anni that Saturday because there had been a storm. This was a prearranged message for the reappearance of Louis.

'Mrs Streiber how is Anni?' she asked breathlessly.

'Anni has a little cold,' Helga said.

'Can you put her on the phone?' Imogen's hand were shaking as she waited, twisting the cord in her hands.

'Mummy, is that you?'

'Yes, darling it's me.'

'Are you coming to see me, this weekend?'

Imogen was tangling the cord so hard around her fingers she was cutting off the blood supply. 'No darling. Mummy has to move house.'

'But, Mummy!' She snuffled. 'You always come on a Saturday.'

It broke Imogen's heart not to see her, but it was too dangerous.

'When I do come I'll bring you something special, how's that?'

When she got back on the phone to Helga Streiber she lowered her voice, 'Helga I need you to listen carefully. I think this time Louis really has found me.'

She heard Mrs Streiber's sharp intake of breath. 'God how?'

'I don't know. I've thought it for a while because someone's been hanging around and following me. What should I do? I'm so worried I can't think straight.'

'Get out,' Helga said. 'Come here and stay a while.'

Imogen was still threading the cord through her fingers. 'I can't, I mean, he could follow me there. I dare not.'

Helga was silent. 'I see your point. However, you can't keep running away from this oaf forever.'

'I realise that.' She was biting her lip. 'Just look after Anni. I'll have to think.' When she put the phone down she pressed her back to the wall and slithering down against it, she burst into tears.

Anni lived with Helga Streiber and it was a good arrangement because she was safer there, away from Louis. Louis had been a crazy man.

Imogen had been modelling lingerie at a classy hotel when she met Louis. She'd had a good job as a supervisor in a lingerie company and one day one of the models had fallen ill. Despite having no desire to be a model, Herr Faltermeyer had asked her to stand in and it had been good money and she found it easy to do. As she'd moved among the tables she'd brushed too close and a man with compelling eyes had touched her thigh. When she'd looked down she was met with a dark intense stare. It was Louis who was grinning at her and smoking a fat cigar. Instantly, she was scared of him, but she had a weakness for powerful men and Louis was sexually compelling. He had thick muscular shoulders and a thick muscular dick to match. After the show he waited outside the changing area and he tailed her until she gave way. She guessed she'd just been too weak and she'd given in to the barrage of flowers and jewellery. Imogen moved in to the fancy apartment he kept permanently in Berlin, and before she knew it she was pregnant with Anni. It shouldn't have happened and it couldn't have come at a worse time, because at last she'd relented and been promoted to be one of the house models.

Late one night, someone called at the apartment and Louis slithered soundlessly out of bed. The nocturnal visits weren't unusual but this time there was a lot of urgent muffled talking. Curious, Imogen pressed her ear to the crack in his study door and listened. Louis was a crook as she'd suspected for a long time and there was muttered talk of a deal involving arms to some country in South America. Her blood ran cold.

Afterwards, she'd sat on the bed her fingers and toes freezing. Yesterday, she'd found out she was pregnant and she'd been about to tell Louis. Now when she heard Louis was evidently into something a bit sinister, she felt sick. How could she bring a kid up with a father like that? Worse still, Louis was so possessive he could be scary and he'd go nuts when he knew she was pregnant. He'd been married before and he loved kids, but his wife had been barren. He craved a large family; he'd often told her about it, held her hand and been very intense staring into her eyes and saying how much he'd idolise a son or daughter. That afternoon she'd packed her bags and left the plush apartment and gone to stay with a friend. Louis found her in no time though, he had contacts everywhere, worse still he'd found out about the fancy gynaecologist she'd gone to and dragged the truth out of him.

She sat in her friend's lounge pleating her fingers whilst Louis strode around like a caged bull. Even when he was like this she still had a sexual weakness for him.

'Come back, Imogen, I'll give you anything you want. Name it.'

'I don't want to come back.'

He dropped to his knees in front of her and he put his hands on her silk stockings, searching under her panties, his finger tickling her in the way she loved. She was wet already.

'You see, babe you can't resist me!'

'No, Louis, I'm scared of you.'

His dark eyes leered at her. 'Scared of me, what the fuck are you on about? Did I ever lay a finger on you? You know I'd never do that.'

Imogen glared at him. 'No, Louis, you didn't, but there's no way I'm bringing a kid up with you.'

'Well, we'll see about that, this is my kid.' He stood up stroking his fingers through his hair. 'And, you needn't try that running away act, 'cause wherever you go I'll find you and I'll find our kid. You two-bit silk stocking fuck whore.'

The words really hurt her. So, that was what he honestly thought of her, was it? There was nothing for it, she left her friend and she moved to Frankfurt. She had a few small savings from the modelling job but they wouldn't last her for long and she'd have to lie low. The apartment block she lived in was a haven for whores. Not bad women but women down on their luck. It was then she thought about turning a trick or two. After all, men had a fascination with her legs and there was nothing guys seemed to like better than coming on her silk stockings, but she could never be a whore and Imogen knew it.

One day, she got a packet in the post and it was from Louis. "I'm following you, whore", it said. "As soon as you have my kid you'd better watch out. I got the contacts and money to find you wherever you are." That night she packed up again and she moved to Berlin. Berlin was huge and she thought she could lose herself there. She worked for awhile as a waitress and when she got bigger she took a job as a seamstress in a small *atelier* and it was here she met Frau Streiber. Imogen had confided in no one, however, she could confide in Helga Streiber because Helga understood. She'd had a mean husband and run away and made a good life for herself. She was now a woman of independent financial means and she had a nice apartment in a really tasteful suburb of Berlin near a beautiful park and good schools. She was the mother Imogen had lost and she was also her best friend. It was Helga's idea to bring up Anni.

As soon as Imogen gave birth she fell in love with the little blonde bundle and she had to admit the apartment in the eastern sector was not an ideal place to bring up a child. For one thing it was far too draughty and whilst it was convenient for work, a lot of unsavoury sorts hung around the dark alleyways and corners and it was full of whores, even more than in the apartment in Frankfurt. In the summer when she wrenched open the windows her evening rang to the accompaniment of the muffled groans and grunts of the women fucking and she had to turn her radio up to drown it out.

Soon, she was living the life of a recluse but it was important to keep a low profile. She knew Louis would stop at nothing to find Anni and for some reason he scared her shitless and she didn't know why. After Anni's birth she got a job dancing and men went crazy over her legs in the silk stockings. She could do a neat routine and her limbs were flexible. Another dancer told her about Karl and Karl liked her and taught her good control over her body. Soon, she was earning reasonable money and Hermann continually began hounding her to apply for a job at a sassy Berlin nightclub. She couldn't take it, of course, because Louis always used to hang out at joints like that and there was always the possibility he would see her, but Hermann did find her the job at the lower class joint, The Blue Palm club.

At the weekend she went down into Herr Eichel's pastry shop and Herr Eichel would give her one or two cakes for Anni. Imogen put on her best dress and her mother's old fur coat and then when it got dark, she'd walk to the tram and take it right the way across town and out into the suburbs to Helga Streiber's. There she stayed the night and the next day she'd take Anni out in her little cream coat and hat and they'd go for a walk in the park and feed the remains of the cakes to the ducks on the pond.

Anni was going to be stunning, Imogen knew that. She had inherited all that was best about the Heinemann line and none of Louis except for his eyes. She had Imogen's thick hair, which she wore coiled up onto her head in two round twists, and huge brown eyes. Those were the eyes which Imogen had fallen in love with, in Louis. They were compelling eyes, eyes able to seduce. Her skin was pale and from the look of it she was going to have a fine pair of legs. One thing was for sure, though, Imogen was going to make sure she didn't know how to use them. Already Anni liked stockings and she copied her mother pulling them on and off and stroking them. But it was child's play and no way would Imogen let it happen. Silk stocking legs attracted guy's like Louis. A silk stocking whore would never attract a good man.

Chapter Six

IMOGEN SAT ON THE bed biting her nails, and then she slipped out to get a bread roll from Herr Eichel's because there was no food in the apartment. When she came back she trod on the envelope which had been slipped beneath the door and she froze. It was the same plain brown envelope she'd received before and she recognised Louis's writing immediately.

Michael sent her flowers although she'd told him not to. They arrived that afternoon as she lay on her bed; a dozen red roses threaded through with baby's breath. Michael had asked her to meet him for coffee and cake at a sweet little café he knew about, but she couldn't, of course, it was out of the question and breaking all the rules she'd set herself about boyfriends. She didn't know what to do.

It came to four o'clock and she stood by the window, considering with her finger to her lip. By now, she could have been having coffee with Michael their legs pleasantly rubbing beneath the table and she felt a sharp pang of misery. She wished he'd forgotten it, not pushed her like this. Why couldn't he have left it at a quick fuck last night? She took the picture of her mother off the mirror and was just putting it in the case and straightening the bedclothes when a knock came at the door.

'Imogen, this is Michael, open up because I know you're in there.'

Imogen sighed. This was the trouble with love; it followed you around like a bad smell. She opened the door a crack.

'Didn't I make myself clear?'

'Sure you did, honey. But I'm Michael Levenstein.' He stuck his foot in the door. 'Open up and let me in unless you want this conversation on the landing.'

She opened the door and closing it behind her she locked it and leant against it. Michael sat on the bed. He made her heart stop and start with that tender way he had of looking at her.

'I figured it out,' he said, patting the bedcover. 'Come and sit here and tell me all about your secret.'

'Michael for heaven's sake,' Imogen said sighing and coming and sitting down so close their arms rubbed together.

'And, what the shit! You going somewhere? You running out on me?' He indicated the cases.

'You don't understand me,' she said, peering at him doubtfully.

'After the way I fucked you last night I think I understand you well enough. As shit crazy as it sounds, I've been and fallen in love with you.'

Imogen felt a warm flush of happiness. 'Oh, that's a big statement.'

Michael took her hand. 'I didn't think I'd ever fall in love so hard. Now, I have and I'm not about to let it go. I'm nearly 38 and love doesn't bite that often.'

'No, no I don't guess it does.' Imogen stroked his finger, which was inching up her hem. She was unable to prevent the warm rush and she wanted it. He feathered her cheek and turning her face towards him fondled her lips with his own and slid his tongue along the inside of her bottom lip, while beginning to unfasten the buttons on her top and running his other finger around the edges of her frilly brassière. She ignited in rapid pulses and her arms came around his neck, Her nipples were alarmingly erect and she was so primed, one touch and she thought she might explode. He got to his knees and pulling down her panties and opening her legs he moved aside the silk stocking chastity belt and began sucking vigorously on her clit.

'Michael don't. I can't think straight,' she objected as she felt the warm spurt of liquid between her legs.

'I don't want you to think straight. I want you to make some kind of rash decision.' He was kissing her face again, hot wet sexy kisses. 'I want you to forget whatever shit stupid idea you have of running out on me and come back to the States so we can get married.'

'Are you crazy!' She tried pushing him away with her hand. 'This is the real world.'

'Yes, honey and I'm not kidding, life's too short.' He pushed her back on the bed, fumbling with his shirt buttons as his hands dropped to his flies. She could see he was already erect.

She lay on the bed with her legs trailing over the side as his hand came under her skirt and he stroked her feverish warm flesh. Imogen's heart was thundering. She felt confused as she touched his face and hair and he closed his eyes.

'Oh, my God.' She gasped as he placed his finger under the stocking chastity belt and winding it, pulled it deliciously tight.

'You didn't take it off, after all.' He winked at her. 'You must have thought I'd come back because you wouldn't go against my wishes, I'm master of the silk stocking and you knew if you did, I'd be mad.'

'I guess I did hope you'd come back, I was being selfish.' She threaded her fingers through his hair.

'Shit, you're something.' He kissed her again and then reaching behind her he loosened her brassière and taking it off he began to kiss and bite her nipples. Imogen groaned and sprawled back against the bed, it was just too good, she thought, as his tongue licked, and began its slow journey south towards her pubic triangle. He began licking it all over and sliding his tongue in and out of her, and she raised her legs and wetting her finger she pulled aside the silk stockings and began to massage her clit. She'd only taken the stockings off to wash and dry them and then she'd put them straight back on for some reason. He was right, she enjoyed the sense of control he had over her and she liked to fantasise over it.

God, his tongue felt good and he took his time, licking and stroking until she felt that first spasm, then he stood over her and she raised her knees and before she could caress him he was using the tip of his cock to gently tease around her hole, wetting himself with her come, lubing himself up. He slid inside her in small controlled increments a little at a time teasing and rotating.

Her hands came into fists and she arched her back. 'That's good, so good.'

Michael began to piston back and forth intent on her pleasure, intent on not just the fuck. 'Open your eyes,' he said.

She did so and as he thrust he kept eye contact, it was deep passionate; it wasn't simply sex. 'I'll prove I love you,' he said.

'What? You're not just in love with my fucking silk stockings then?'

'Imogen, for God sake don't talk like that.' He pressed his finger to her lips. 'When you talk like that, it only makes me hornier.' She came with her muscles flexing around him, pushing up and grinding his tool inside her, then she flopped back aching for it and Michael slid out. He took the silk stocking she'd given him out of his pocket and he wound it tightly around his stem, squeezing the blood into the bulbous tip of his cock to prevent his ejaculation before opening her legs wide and holding his tool in his hands, he began rubbing it back and forth up her silk clad thigh. She watched him mesmerised with her finger in her thatch, bringing herself to orgasm again but slowly this time, grinding her teeth as she enjoyed the sensitivity of the second rollercoaster ride of pleasure. Michael watched her finger and as it moved he moved his cock so she felt like she was fucking him in lots of ways.

'I've got a better idea,' she said. 'I'll sit on you and you can fuck my legs. I'll open them just enough like this and you can go up and down. Lie down, Michael.'

Michael lay down on the bed and Imogen sat on top of him holding herself above him with her arms. Spreading his legs, she grabbed his cock and pulling it up between her own she squeezed her thighs around his meaty tool. Michael shuddered and said, 'Oh shit.' He gradually began to raise himself up and down enjoying the friction of the silk stockings and Imogen watched his penis head, wet and ripe now moving up and down. When he couldn't bear it any longer she tumbled off him and ripping off the silk stocking cock ring she brought her head down and fucked him with her mouth.

Michael's cheeks were pink and beads of perspiration were standing out on his forehead, he gasped and shook and eventually cried out, 'Dear shit, Lord.'

Imogen laughed, it was the first gut laugh she'd had in ages.

She didn't leave, she lay curled up with Michael, one hand under her cheek while he stroked her hair. The air was heavy with sex.

'So, babe, what are you running away from?' He ran his finger under the silk stocking chastity belt.

'It's a long story, Michael.'

'OK, however, I think it's about time you told me, don't you?' Michael touched her lips, her teeth and she closed her eyes and vibrated.

He was silent for a while, then his hands came up to her nipples and she held them there and moved his fingers over them, encouraging him to pinch her gently.

'Start at the beginning.'

She rolled over and Michael ran his fingers along her wet

silk stockings as she parted her legs inviting him into her thatch. His constant fiddling seemed to take her mind off what she had to tell him.

'I fell in love with a bastard and a crook, a very rich man, but well things happened, I ran away, I was penniless. He always called me a whore and I am a whore, I must be because I almost did it, I almost went on the streets.'

'You needed a good reason to do that. More than running away from a man you were scared of. What was it, darling, tell me?'

'One night, I didn't even have the marks for a dry bread roll. I'm ashamed to say it, but I put on a cheap coat and high heeled shoes and cheap seamed stockings - as it seemed blasphemy to casually fuck a guy in real silk – and I walked out onto the streets. I must have been born for a life of sin, because so many men approached me and followed me like I was a bitch on heat. I thought I can do this; I can do what I never thought I could do, since it's for a good reason. The trouble is I couldn't go through with it.'

'A bread roll would be as good a reason as any,' Michael said suspiciously. 'And what the hell – you didn't actually do it anyway, so what's the problem?'

Her eyes beaded with tears. They welled up and it was more than she could do to hold them back. 'Oh, Michael, there's more.' Her fingers coaxed his nipples and slid down to his hard cock. 'I'd tell you, but I'm afraid you'd run away, all men run away.'

'I'm Michael Levenstein and I'm not about to run away. You can tell me anything.' He grabbed hold of her, kissing her deeply and Imogen pressed her lips to his and her tongue thrust inside greedily, caressing and feathering his mouth.

She was quiet a moment. 'I have a daughter called Anni.' She held her breath; she could feel Michael's warm heartbeat. 'So, you see how impossible things are?'

'Where is she, where's your daughter?'

'She stays with a good friend of mine, Frau Helga

Streiber.'

Michael was winding his fingers through her hair. 'And you see her, do you? Why isn't Anni here?' His fingers were continuing to pluck and fondle.

'It's a long story. But, when I came to Berlin I met Helga Streiber and she was very kind to me. As you can see this is a shit place and no place for a kid, she took Anni and said she'd look after her.'

Imogen's heart was thumping harder than ever, as she stared at Michael. 'So now everything I do is for Anni. I save all the money I can and I put it into a bank account. So you see how it was, Michael. It wasn't just about a bread roll. I thought I could fuck anyone if it meant I could take care of Louis's little girl. I'd murder for Anni, but I couldn't, because you see, you see … sex without love is nothing and I couldn't do it, I might be a silk stocking whore but I'm not a cunt whore. Although, Louis called me his cunt whore.'

A tear rolled down her cheek and he trapped it. Then Michael slithered down the bed and Imogen rested her heels on his shoulders. He stroked the silk stockings very slowly with his hands and then he kissed them and unclipping her suspenders he rolled them down. Imogen shivered, it was a slow shiver which started in her toes and spread up over her body to the tips of her hair.

'Imogen, you know something, I don't care a fuck what you did or, who you were. I don't care a flying fuck.'

She was holding her breath as Michael gradually eased the silk stockings down her leg kissing each inch of flesh as he went, propelling the spiralling warmth up out of her in delicious satisfying ripples.

'Michael, what are you doing?'

'It occurs to me I never saw you without them.' He took one off, stroking her foot with his fingers and tickling the sole so she stretched and tingled with pleasure.

'You know something.' He grinned, 'You're one sexy lady, you silk stocking whore. But, I want to try this out. I need to see if I still get the same kick from this sexy bare leg. He began to roll down the other silk stocking, and gradually, very gradually began to kiss his way all the way up.

Imogen groaned, a fire was growing now, a tantalising cunt fire and she reached down and spread her fingers through her thatch and teased herself. 'Michael, ah Michael.' It was too much to bear, this rising tide of, not just passion, but something else – dare she call it love? 'Oh my God, Michael.' He drew her up and onto his knees and while he stroked and held her thighs she lowered herself onto his pole. Then Michael began unknotting the silk stocking chastity belt and threw it onto the bed. 'I don't think we need that any more, do you?'

'Michael I ..?'

He put his fingers on her lips.

'Enough, we'll talk about it later.'

She buried her mouth in his fine blond hair and as she moved up and down Michael put his fingers between her butt cheeks and he butt fucked her. The pleasure rose in unimaginable spirals and her orgasm came with butt clenching fury. She cried out, not from pain but pleasure.

'Hey, it wasn't that bad, was it?'

'No, it was perfect.'

'Well then, Mrs Silk Stocking?'

'Don't joke, Michael.'

'I'm not. Tomorrow you can wave goodbye to this flea pit and I'll move you into the Adlon Kempinski Hotel.'

'My God, you can't.'

'Sure I can.'

'If Louis is tailing me, he'd find me there. It's on the Unter den Linden, he used to go there all the time to meet his business associates. I can't do that. He'd threaten me, he's always called me a whore and God knows, he'll take Anni away from me.'

Michael squeezed her hand. 'That shit heads not scaring

me; you'll be safe with me, besides I want to meet Anni. Hell, if you're that scared we can get dressed and we can get a car and go and get Anni right this minute. I'll shoot the bastard if he tries to take her off you.'

She shook her head. 'No Michael, it's very sweet, but you don't know Louis.' She moistened her lips. 'I'm scared. Last night, I got a letter. I think Louis as been having me watched for weeks. Adele Weinberger upstairs is sure she's seen him. If he knows that much about me he might already suspect where Anni is. He'd find her.'

'He can't take her, baby.'

'Yes, yes he can, Michael. He can do anything. He thinks I'm a whore.'

'And from what you tell me he's just a two-bit crook. Show me the letter!'

Imogen clambered off the bed and going to her locked jewellery box she sprung the catch and came back carrying the letter. Her fingers were trembling as if the letter burnt. She held it out and he took it. He skimmed the words and his eyes normally so blue, so cool, became hard like ice. She could imagine how Michael Levenstein would look in the courtroom.

'The guy's trying to frighten you that's all.'

She crawled onto the bed. 'You don't understand Louis, he killed people. I know you'll say it's not true but I know he did. He's capable of anything.'

'So what, the dude killed people.' Michael folded the letter, then he cupped her cheek and she pressed her lips into his hand. 'This isn't a movie and it's not that easy to kidnap people. Don't worry, baby. Tomorrow I'll ring my brother in Seattle, he's a good lawyer and specialises in family law. He'll know what to do and if he doesn't I'll get father on the line. Then, hell, we'll get you out of here.'

A lump came into Imogen's throat, her hands were shaking. 'You'd do that for me?'

'Baby, I'm gonna do it. This moment.' Michael smiled

and this time his smile was powerful and sweet and she saw another side to handsome Michael Levenstein and it was strong and sexy and she liked it. Her head swam pleasantly.

'And if I need it I've got the power of the entire Levenstein family behind me. Now, babe come here.' He held out his arms, and looping the stocking around her neck he drew her mouth down onto his. Imogen spread her legs over his narrow hips and she felt his cock press into her mound with a pleasant persistence.

'I don't think your family would like me much,' she said. 'I hardly think they'll be happy having a silk stocking whore in the family.'

Michael laughed. 'We may be Levensteins but we're grafters and we come from tough stock. You'd like my family, Imogen, and they'd like you.'

'Why, do I believe you?' she replied, thrumming with ecstasy as she trailed her fingers across his face. 'I do believe you.'

'Here's the plan.' Michael whispered.

Chapter Seven

IMOGEN DRESSED, SHE PUT on her simple blue dress and her string of pearls but for the first time she didn't bother with the silk stockings. Next, she called Helga Streiber and taking a car, they drove out to the suburbs.

Helga had already dressed Anni in her cream coat and she wore a pair of pink stockings and buckled shoes. As they sat in the car she played with Imogen's earrings and her face was glowing. She looked, Michael thought, adorable and just like her mama. He took them shopping and he bought her and Anni some new dresses and shoes and he never let her out of his sight. Gradually the fear left Imogen – maybe if Louis had been watching he'd been scared away. Michael bought her a square deco diamond engagement ring and then he bought tickets for New York.

Once, a long time ago, Imogen had walked through the same lounge of the Adlon Kempinski Hotel with Louis, in a pair of very high heels and in a fine silk dress and fine silk stockings, but that seemed a long time ago.

That night, they celebrated their engagement whilst Helga Streiber babysat Anni in their sumptuous suite.

Imogen felt like she was in a dream as she stared at Michael across the table. He'd asked for a small table, he'd been very specific and as she tried to eat her soup he slipped his hand up and down her legs, which were dressed now in the finest silk stockings money could buy. Upstairs, just for a laugh, he'd filled her make-up bag with Cervin.

He fucked her sensuously, his finger pressed into her cunt and a deadpan expression on his face. Occasionally he stroked her suspender belt, back and forth, before moving from cunt to suspender. Her spoon dropped with a rattle when she orgasmed and everyone looked. 'Whoops.'

'Whoops.' Michael leaned over the table.

'Well, ain't this a pretty sight?' Louis said.

Imogen was so startled she knocked over her glass of champagne spilling it on the white tablecloth. Her hand flew to her mouth and the blood drained from her face.

'So, the stocking whore's returned to her nesting place. You know, babe you always looked best in chic surroundings. I think there's something classy about a sexy whore who hides it under the table.'

She had not broken her gaze with Michael who had now surreptitiously removed his cunt wet finger from under the table and whose eyes were like shards of ice in his handsome face.

'Well, holy shit if it isn't Louis Berner. I've been waiting to make your acquaintance Mr Berner,' Michael said coldly.

Never had Imogen loved Michael more than in that moment as he sat back assuredly in his chair, before pushing it out a fraction he crossed his legs and hands over his belly and considered Louis coolly.

Louis, who was chewing on his customary cigar, stopped the movements of his mouth. He was surprised and no wonder, because Louis wasn't used to being answered back.

'What the hell?' he said finally, grabbing hold of Michael's collar and pulling him to his feet so he could stare in his face. 'Who the fuck do you think you're talking to?'

Imogen was on her feet and her heart was thumping. 'Louis, let him go, this isn't worth it.'

'And that goes for you too, you whore. Who do you think you're talking to?'

Imogen's lips trembled. By now everyone had noticed what was going on and they'd all stopped eating so they could watch the free entertainment. Louis's grip was tightening.

'Well Imogen, you sure surprise me, 'cause I sure as hell didn't think you went for pretty boys.'

Michael's more of a man than you'll ever be,' Imogen said. 'You inhabit the sewers, Louis, that's where you come from. You and your dirty money.' Tears were stinging her eyes.

'I've come to get my daughter,' Louis said turning his attention to Imogen. 'Where is she? 'Cause I'm taking her home. There ain't no way on this earth I'm leaving her with her whoring mummy. Is this how you do it, babes? You go for men who can wine and dine you. Nice society men. How much you charging him?'

Imogen's lips trembled. 'How dare you!'

Louis had loosened his hold on Michael as two waiters headed their way. He straightened his tie. 'Well, I guess I'll be seeing you in court then?'

Imogen looked at Michael who was stroking down his collar; he didn't seem at all perturbed.

'I've seen a whole lot of guys like you, Mr Berner, so I won't press charges,' he said succinctly. 'Why don't you head on out of Dodge peacefully. Imogen's not yours to worry about, come here, Imogen.' He held out his hand and Imogen came around the table. Michael put his hand around her waist. 'Perhaps you'll say sorry to the future Mrs Levenstein.'

Louis burst into laughter. 'You're pulling my leg. You telling me you're marrying this cunt whore?'

'Sure, I love her and I'm marrying her, so if you want to take on the whole Levenstein family including my father Abel Levenstein, you're welcome.'

Louis stared for a moment and his cheeks turned red. 'You're kidding me, you can't be that Levenstein? How on God's earth could a Levenstein go as low as to end up with this tart?'

Michael was stroking her butt with sensuous back and forward sweeps of his hand. When she looked at him, he

70

was cool, cool and strong and she loved him more than ever.

'I'm that Levenstein,' he said. 'And, I'd crawl through the sewers for this tart.'

Louis glanced at the waiters again, and then he stared at Imogen before he pointed his large thumb at her. 'You realise you ain't heard the last of this?'

Imogen said nothing.

Chapter Eight

LATER, SHE WAS SITTING on the edge of Anni's bed and Michael came and leant against the doorframe, he was holding a glass of champagne. Imogen kissed her daughter's forehead and then, strolling over to Michael, she stepped out into the suite's sumptuous lounge quietly pulling the door up behind her. 'Am I totally free of Louis?' she asked, as taking the champagne she sipped it.

Michael was wriggling the peach lace peignoir he'd bought her that afternoon, up her leg and circling her skin with his thumb.

'I'm thinking he could be a bug flying around our heads for awhile but he hasn't got anything on you.' Michael grinned. 'My brother telephoned me this afternoon. I was going to keep what he said for when I was fucking you and we were just about to get to the high point in the proceedings, but I can't wait.'

'You dog.' She wound her arms around his neck and Michael slid his finger into the slit between her butt cheeks and teased her hole.

'Apparently, Louis Berner has a list of petty crimes so long I could nail him tomorrow, but I don't think he wants that. I reckon he'll keep his head down from now on. No one wants to tangle with a Levenstein.' He studied her lips before touching them with his finger.

'Thank God.' Imogen replied, relaxing as her body folded around him.

'You're one hell of a beautiful silk stocking whore, do you know that?'

'If any other guy said that to me now I'd string his balls up.' She narrowed her eyes teasingly. 'I may even string up his balls with my silk stockings.'

'That sounds good to me. How would you do that? Describe it to me in graphic detail. How hard and how tight?' He was laughing as he pushed his finger further inside her and Imogen shivered in warm orgasmic bliss, combing her hands through his thick hair.

'Am I safe now, Michael, really safe?'

'Sure you're safe, you and Anni. Now, show me you Cervin bitch, show me how tight you'd bind me with those silk stockings.'

Her hand moved downwards and she began working his flies, before coming inside and against his bare testicles with slow determined purpose. The thrill of sex felt even better now, better because she was free to fly with her emotions and she didn't feel as if she was held in such tightly stretched, mental bondage by Louis. A warmth blossomed inside her, which was more than orgasm, it was intense burning ecstasy, melting away the last droplets of icy fear. She ran across the lounge and into their bedroom, and putting down her champagne class and dragging open the bedside drawer she picked up a handful of her Cervin stockings, waving them in front of him. 'I'm about to show you how tight Michael. Something like this.'

Raising her arms she stripped off the peignoir, letting it slither to the floor with the hiss of exaggerated silk.

'Holy Moses!' Michael's gaze flickered over her naked curves as she sashayed around him. 'Wow.' She'd creamed her legs and shaved her pubic thatch and she stood in front of him dressed in just her silk suspenders and as usual, her silk Cervin stockings. Imogen pushed Michael back against the wall, rubbing her crotch against his pant leg. When their lips met, the embrace was hot and wet and it was all to the accompaniment of Michael's finger dancing in and out of her hole again as she ground her pelvis against his ramrod hard cock.

'I'd tie them up so tight you'd scream … do you really want me to describe to you what I'd do next, or would you rather I showed you?' Imogen's hand was curling over his thrusting cock. Smoothing a stocking between her fingers, she ran her tongue over the naked silk and tying it expertly around Michael's balls she led him towards the bed.

Imogen unbuttoned his fine crisp white shirt, and kissing his rigid nipples she slithered down his body and licking his skin, wriggled his pants down over his hips. His cock was near her mouth and Michael was trembling.

'Show me, darling,' Michael croaked huskily, pulling her backwards towards the bed. 'Show me how it's gonna be, married to a silk stocking whore. But, you sure as hell can't wear me out, remember, 'cause we've got that early flight first thing tomorrow.' Michael's hand was on one of her silk stockings and Imogen dropped to her knees between his legs, kissing his balls with dancing feather-like motions of her lips and her tongue before she began winding the Cervin stocking tighter and tighter. Michael was laughing, however, his face had become serious and intent. 'Oh, I see what you mean.'

'Tighter?' she asked.

'Yes, tighter. Fuck me with those silk stockings, babe.'

Imogen attached the one Cervin to another and tying it around his waist she fashioned Michael a chastity belt. The belt pulled his balls back and high and they squeezed pleasurably.

'Well, well,' Michael teased. 'Mrs Levenstein, I do believe you've made me my own chastity belt. You surely are a silk stocking whore aren't you?'

Imogen's tongue balanced on her lips, she was shaking with excitement as she tightened the silk stockings even more so Michael's cock and balls were neatly presented for her tongue. 'Tight enough for you, baby?'

'No, keep going.' He was staring at her as his breath

came in short static gasps, and she drowned in the intensity of that look which said, "I love you Imogen." Michael eased the combs out of her hair and the blond cascade tumbled over her shoulders as Imogen started winding yet another silk stocking tighter and tighter around his pole.

'How does that feel?'

'Like I'm on fire.' Michael sat down on the bed with a grunt and Imogen's tongue darted out to gather the drop of precome on his tip. Imogen guessed a tight silk stocking wound so tightly around something as sensitive as a cock was bound to make any man excited. She eased him into her mouth and slid her tongue up and down and around before biting the turgid stem; teasing it and flicking her tongue against the tip.

'I should make you pay for that,' he said.

'You can make me pay later.' Her hands moved around and she cupped his buttocks, jerking on the silk stocking as she did so. The sensation made him groan with pleasure. She loved the taste of him, the feel of him as he began to rock in and out of her mouth and the best part was, it was going to go on for some time, well at least until she let him take off the silk stockings chastity belt. Michael stretched back on the bed, drawing her down onto his hard muscular body.

'Mrs Levenstein, I adore you. Now tell me how many naughty silk stocking whore tricks you know?'

'Plenty. But, for now I just want to love you, Michael.'

She traced his lips with her finger, kissing him deeply, deliciously, whilst his rigid cock forced its way between her legs and began nuzzling her greedy moist place. He was beginning the slow dance and the rigid tip felt achingly good nuzzling inside her, sliding in and out as she lifted her leg and coiled it around him and drew him even deeper inside; the stocking clad balls hard against her groin. She giggled, tweaking one with her fingers.

Michael breathed hotly in her ear as their slick bodies began to move with a newer more urgent kind of friction. He loved her in many different ways as she tumbled on the bedclothes and the arching wave of ecstasy rose and fell and rose again and always her hand was on the silk stocking chastity belt, loosening it and tightening it as she controlled the pleasure.

It was only when he was thrusting gently with his hands squeezing hard into her buttocks she realised she wanted him now and completely and she loosened the silk stocking bondage to allow the warm throbbing explosion high up inside her. It was all the things she'd dreamt about but not dared hope for; a clenching swirling spasm of bliss as she tightened around him and her whole body seemed to gather him in

'God, I love you Michael Levenstein,' she murmured softly.

Afterwards, she spread out naked on the bed, stretching each of her limbs languorously. I thought there was only one kind of man to be caught by a silk stocking cocktease, she pondered as Michael's hand crept under her stocking and he began kissing her crotch. She'd always be a silk stocking whore but she'd nailed one hell of a fine man with a pair of Cervin.

The Lord of Summer
by Jenna Bright

Chapter One

'WELL, I GUESS THIS is it.' With relief, Gemma Parker lowered the box she carried from her aching arms, down to the sun baked earth that surrounded the Green Man pub. Stretching her hands up over her head, she gazed around her as she wiggled to unknot her spine after four hours in the car. Across the bridge, just behind the pub building, verdant green forest stretched all the way to the horizon. But on this side of the riverbank all Gem could see were dead petunias, browning grass, and dusty banks down to the trickle of water that ran under the rickety wood of the bridge. That, and the tired, brick building of the pub itself, windows obscured by sun bleached wooden boards. 'Home sweet home. Apparently.'

Lowering her arms to her sides, she squinted up at the pub sign, swinging from its metal brackets in the sunshine. It wasn't a design she'd seen before; a man's face, handsome and tan, but with leaves and vines surrounding his head, making up his hair, curling around his cheeks and under his chin. The Green Man himself, she supposed.

The sun pounded down against her back, freakishly hot even for July in England. Gem tugged at her sleeveless white blouse where it stuck to her skin, and ran a hand over the sweat-damp hair at the nape of her neck. Her skin felt sticky, overheated, as if it were too tight for her body. Her thighs, bare under her skirt, caught against each other whenever they touched, dragging skin against skin. Gem's tongue peeked out to moisten her lips; the air hung heavy, muggy. As if it were waiting for a storm. And her whole body seemed to have caught the feeling.

At least the pub might be cool inside. And their first delivery was due that afternoon. They could get set up, get the fridges to temperature, then crack open an icy bottle of beer this evening to wash away the day. Maybe christen the bar the way they always did, the first night in a new pub.

Her husband, Dan, leant a suitcase up against one of the picnic tables on the river bank and scowled. 'God, what a dump. They seriously want us to turn this place round?'

'That's what Mark said.' Gem bit the inside of her cheek as she recalled the conversation. The culmination of six months spent deflecting Mark Fisher's advances, and it had resulted in them being sent to the back of beyond, to run the least profitable pub ever in the Fisher Breweries chain. At least Dan hadn't heard the things Mark had said to her. If he had, they wouldn't have jobs at all, she was sure of that. Her husband had a temper, when it mattered.

'Who do they expect us to sell beer to, out here? Bambi and his friends!' Dan made a disgusted noise, and turned back towards the car. Leaning against the picnic table, Gem watched him make his way down the hill to the tiny car park, his shoulders wide and wonderful under his T-shirt, his worn jeans clinging to the curve of his arse. No doubt about it, her husband was a gorgeous man.

A gorgeous man with a jealous streak a mile wide.

She shook her head, as Dan reached into the boot for another box. She'd known who he was when she married him, and she'd taken it on willingly. After all, why would she want another man when she had Dan? So what did it matter if he frightened away any guy who tried to talk to her?

Only, Dan's usual methods hadn't worked with Mark

Fisher. He was their boss, for a start, and not the sort of man to be scared off by a warning look and Dan's arm around her waist. He sincerely believed he could steal Gem away from her husband, for as long as he was likely to want her. He was wrong, of course, and Gem had told him so a thousand times.

He just hadn't listened.

Which was how Gem had found herself backed into the corner of the basement of their old pub, The Golden Eagle, with Mark reaching for the buttons of her blouse.

In retrospect, she probably hadn't needed to knee him in the groin *and* bash him over the head with the cocktail shaker serendipitously placed on the shelf beside her. One or the other would have sufficed.

But it sure had felt good.

Right up until the phone call announcing their move from the popular, trendy, city centre Golden Eagle to the rural, derelict Green Man. And Dan's angry confusion about why.

'Fisher Breweries' Managers of the Year three years running, and they stick us *here,*' Dan said, bringing up the last of their luggage. 'I don't know what Mark Fisher's thinking.'

But Gemma did. And she knew she could never, never tell her husband.

Because somewhere, deep inside, a very small part of her was afraid he wouldn't believe her. Working behind the bar, flirting was part of the job, however much Dan didn't like it. And he'd always been suspicious of the way she'd smiled at Mark, been pleasant to him – before he started his campaign of seduction. She'd tried explaining that it was just good business sense – if a few smiles for the boss kept their pub in favour with the brewery, what did it hurt? But Dan had never seen it that way.

What if he didn't see it her way now? What if he thought she'd led Mark on?

Gem bit her lip. It was ridiculous. Dan trusted her, and

loved her. He'd believe her, of course he would.

She just wasn't quite ready to put that to the test yet.

Dan watched his wife's hips move under her light summer skirt as she swept the floor of their temporary home. The place might look a little better now he'd prised the boards from the windows, and Gem had started cleaning, but still. No way they were staying, he told himself, as Gem brushed her dark hair out of her eyes with her fingers, pushing damp strands behind her ear. Never mind the dust, the heat and the location. Something about the whole situation didn't stack up. Fisher Breweries would never send their best team into the middle of nowhere without good reason.

Something was going on, and Dan needed to know what it was.

Especially if, as he suspected, it had something to do with his wife.

'Tell me again,' he said, leaning against the bar. 'What exactly did Mark say when he told you the brewery wanted us here?'

Gem didn't look at him. A clear sign, right there. Dan's heart clenched inside his chest. She was hiding something.

'He just said that, since the Golden Eagle was running so well, the brewery felt our talents could be better used bringing another pub up to scratch.'

That was rubbish, Dan knew it. No way Fisher Breweries would risk the Golden Eagle losing any of its income generating potential. No way could they really expect them to make a go of the Green Man. And no way Mark Fisher didn't have an ulterior motive. Slimy gits like him always did. Dan just needed to figure out what it was. So, what did Mark want, more than anything?

A cold shard of suspicion pierced his heart, as Dan realised he already knew the answer to that question. Mark wanted what he'd always wanted, from the moment he and Gem had arrived at their first Fisher Breweries pub.

Mark wanted Gem. Dan saw it in every look his boss gave her, every time he visited the Eagle. That desperate desire. God, he'd even offered Dan a better pub for a night with his wife, once, after too many beers. Dan had taken it as a joke, and Mark had laughed, and it had been forgotten.

But what if it hadn't been entirely a joke? What if this was a threat: give me what I want, or you'll be stuck in the back of beyond forever?

The thought was unbearable. Dan shook his head to try and get rid of it, but it clung on in the back of his mind. 'You're sure that's all Mark said?' he asked, trying to understand what was happening here.

Gem spun round, her cheeks flushed from the heat or her anger, Dan wasn't entirely sure. She let the broom drop, crashing against a table, and shoved her hair out of her eyes again. With her colour high and her eyes flashing ... Dan felt a jolt of lust shoot through his body. No wonder Mark wanted her. Dan sure had married a stunning woman.

'Do you think I'm lying to you?' Gem stepped closer, both hands on hips now, emphasising the curve of her waist, the swell of her breasts above ... *Focus, Dan. Serious moment, here.* What was it about this place? Was it the heat, or the remoteness? All he could think about was stripping that shirt from Gem's body.

'I just want to be sure I have all the information,' Dan said, managing to keep his voice mostly even.

Gem's mouth fell open, as if she were about to respond, but then it snapped shut again. Her right cheek dipped in, and Dan knew she was biting down on whatever she'd been about to say. She twisted slightly, turning towards the wall, and her eyes seemed to catch on something there, staring. *What's she looking at?* he wondered, but the curiosity faded when Gem turned back to face him again.

Her eyes still flashed, but not with anger. Her hands slid lower on her hips, cocked to one side. She bit her lip, and Dan swallowed, hard, as she stepped closer. God, he loved her like this.

'Come on, love,' she said, her voice rich and promising. 'It's our first night in our new home.' She was right before him, now, one hand reaching up to brush along his arm, up to his collar. Dan felt a shiver on his skin as her fingers skirted down his chest, tugging up the hem of his T-shirt. 'You don't really want to waste time fighting, do you? Not when we've got a tradition to uphold.'

Dan looked at his beautiful wife, her grey eyes wide, pupils blown. There was something strange going on, and she knew what it was. But right then, Dan didn't give a damn about Mark Fisher, or the Green Man, or anything except getting his wife naked, as quickly as possible.

It'll keep, he told himself, and pulled Gem close.

Gem couldn't explain it. She'd been keyed up, feeling as if her skin were too sensitive, too eager for touch, ever since they'd arrived at the Green Man. But she could honestly say that right then, with Dan's question – accusation, maybe – ringing in her ears, sex was the last thing on her mind. Fear, perhaps. Anger; with him for not trusting her, with Mark for putting her in this position in the first place. Even with herself, because she'd known this would happen, eventually. She hadn't married a stupid man.

She'd been ready to fight back, ready to yell, to distract, to accuse – whatever it took to lead Dan away from the truth. But then …

A carving on the wall; smooth, dark wood had caught her eye. She'd stared, just for a moment or two, taking in the curve of the face, the laughing eyes surrounded by leaves and stems and flowers. *Just like the pub sign.*

And when she'd turned back to Dan, the comeback she'd prepared died on her lips and suddenly her blood was beating with want.

She stepped closer, her body swaying with her desire, watching as his eyes darkened. Reaching out, she ran her fingers up his arm, the feel of his skin under hers enough to make her heart race. And her words, when they came, weren't angry, or defensive, or anything but seductive.

'You don't really want to waste time fighting, do you? Not when we've got a tradition to uphold.'

That was all it took.

Dan's arm snaked around her waist, pulling her tight against him, crushing her breasts to his chest. He lowered his mouth to hers, and she felt her nipples tightening as his other hand ran up her middle, popping open the buttons of her shirt. 'I suppose there are some more important things we could be doing,' he said, and the rasp in his voice made her shiver.

She loved this, loved him. Lived for the feel of his hands on her body, his lips on her neck. How could he think anyone else would ever measure up?

'Far more important,' she murmured, leaning her head back to allow him better access to her throat. His kisses burned a line down from her jaw to her breasts, nuzzling her bra out of the way. She gasped as his lips surrounded a nipple, licking and sucking and tugging as she felt herself growing wet and desperate.

Time to regain some control, Gem decided.

Reaching down, she ran her nails up Dan's thighs, knowing the pressure through the thick denim of his jeans always drove him wild. As she reached the top of his legs, Dan broke away from her breasts and spun her round so her back hit wood. 'Not yet,' he said, wrapping his hands over her hips to lift her up onto the polished surface of the bar. 'I've got plans for you.'

Without giving her time to wonder what plans, Dan slid his palms down her thighs, only to push her skirt up around her waist, out of the way. Gem leant back on her hands, eyes half closed in anticipation. She knew what came next, could almost feel his mouth on her already. Even without everything else that was wonderful about him, the things his tongue could do were more than enough to make marriage to Dan blissful.

Head tipped back, Gem's eyelids fluttered down as Dan ran his tongue along the line of her already soaked underwear. His fingers moved in closer, tugging them down her legs, and she kicked them away. His mouth was instantly back between her thighs, and she felt the hum of his appreciative moan buzz through her. Why had they been fighting again? What could possibly matter except this? Her ponytail hung down along her back, tickling her skin where her shirt had fallen away. Dan had unhooked her bra, she realised, and it hung loose from her arms. She shrugged the rest of the fabric aside, swallowing hard as Dan licked into her. No distractions. She wanted to focus on what her husband was doing to her body.

The tip of his tongue circled around her clit and Gem let out a moan, her head rolling to the side as her body shivered with need. For a moment, she caught a glimpse of her reflection in the window at the end of the bar; her breasts, freed from her bra, thrust out into the humid air, and Dan, bent between her legs, her skirt pushed up between them. Gem smiled. She looked … wanton.

Then the light changed, or the air moved, or something else that Gem couldn't begin to explain. Because she wasn't looking at herself, any more. She was watching a man, outside the pub, on the bridge, just beyond the window. Watching her.

Her moan echoed through the empty pub, and Dan chuckled as he stretched one long finger inside her. 'God, you're wet,' he murmured against the skin of her thigh.

She was, Gem knew. She could feel it. And she knew it wasn't entirely due to Dan's usual good work. The idea that there was someone out there, someone watching her, watching them … 'God, I need you inside me,' she said, and Dan slid up her body, arms behind her shoulders as he said, 'You have all the good ideas.'

He stripped off her skirt as he lowered her from the bar, and she realised that somehow she was completely naked, while Dan was still fully dressed. 'This doesn't seem very fair,' she said, gesturing to the messy pile of her clothes on the floor.

'I'll make it up to you,' Dan promised, as he laid her out on one of the pub tables she'd scrubbed clean that afternoon.

A table right in front of the window she'd just been looking through.

Throbbing heat flooded through Gem's body, every inch of her aching with want. 'Now,' she said, looking up at Dan through a haze of lust. He wasn't smiling or laughing any more. His eyes looked every bit as desperate as she felt.

He didn't bother stripping his clothes, an economy of time Gem appreciated, given the way her blood was pounding. Instead, he yanked open his jeans, pulled out his already hard cock and moved towards her, his rough hands spreading her legs so wide they ached. As he pressed into her, stretching and filling her, Gem felt the incredible tension inside her strain and break with the relief of having him at last. As if it had been years, instead of days, since they'd last made love.

But then, of course, a new need, a new want started to build, as Dan began to move.

With every thrust, Gem felt her body tightening, her breath growing shallower. The familiar spiral up and up and up through every sensation her body could handle, until she reached the top and flew. Except, this time, the pinnacle seemed too far away, out of reach.

'Are you ...' Dan asked, and Gem bit her lip, reaching down between their bodies, rather than tell him no.

Unable to prop herself up with only one arm, she lay flat back on the table, her eyes automatically drawn to the dark glass of the window. Out there, in the night, was there really someone watching? Could he see her right now, spread naked on the warm wood, her husband pounding into her?

Could he see her hand on her breast, pinching at her nipple? Her other hand, lost between her thighs, stroking herself until her body hummed the way it needed to?

That was better. Closer. Just thinking of the man on the bridge, watching ...

A jolt of lust spiked through her body as she thought, *What if he came in?*

What if he wasn't just watching?

Her eyes fluttered closed again on a moan, and Dan picked up speed, rightly assuming she was growing closer. The throbbing feel of her husband inside her kicked her heartbeat up another notch until it was racing. But behind closed eyelids, Gem saw more than just Dan, gripping her hips so tight she'd have bruises.

She saw her watcher, stepping up behind her, cold hands running across her breasts, circling her nipples with a wintery touch, blissful in the midsummer heat. God, she could almost feel him bending to kiss her neck, cool lips making her shiver as Dan kept moving inside her, her hips rising to meet him, each thrust bringing her closer to the top. And then, one icy finger tracing a line down her body, through the curls between her legs, to where she and Dan were joined ...

With one last twist of her own fingers on her clit, Gem felt her body contract and stretch, shuddering as she reached the heights at last and flew. Her mind blurred with sensation, too much feeling to hold a thought, and her eyes closed, unable to cope with vision just then. Her other hand reached out, grabbing Dan's bicep hard as he thrust once, twice, three times more and let out a familiar yell, before dropping down to cover her body with his.

'God, Gem that was ...' He nuzzled against her neck, his skin damp with sweat, and just for a moment, Gem longed for the cool, dry touch of her fantasy watcher.

'Yeah,' she said, eyes drifting towards the window. 'It really was.'

Chapter Two

MORNING BROKE HOTTER THAN ever. Gemma shoved aside the thin sheet Dan had draped over them the night before, and focussed on breathing in the soupy air. Beside her, Dan was still passed out, sweating in his sleep, radiating warmth against her. How were they supposed to work in this heat? There was so much to do to make the pub habitable, let alone profitable, and Dan wanted to open as soon as possible, she knew, and ...

And she didn't care. Gem let her eyes flutter closed as she admitted the truth to herself.

It wasn't the pub that had kept her awake all night. It wasn't even the heat. It was the memory of eyes through a window, and the cold touch of imaginary hands on her body.

She shivered, even in the sweltering air. For a moment last night, a long, wonderful, sensual moment, she had wanted someone else in her marriage. Another man, touching her. Not instead of Dan, never that, but alongside. The two of them, playing her body, making it sing.

When had Dan stopped being enough for her?

No. She couldn't think like that. She loved Dan with all her heart. There was no room for anyone else between them. It was a fantasy. A harmless imagining, always destined to remain just that. Nothing at all to worry about.

And Dan never needed to know what she thought about when they made love, did he? Just like he never needed to know what Mark Fisher had tried to do.

Too many secrets in this marriage. The thought floated in on the heavy air, and Gem tried to ignore it.

Downstairs, the pub phone rang. Glad of the distraction, Gem wrapped the sweat-dampened sheet around her body, leaving Dan sprawled naked across the mattress, and padded out to answer it.

'The Green Man pub,' she said, her voice husky. 'Gemma speaking.'

'Just the person I was looking for.' A shudder ran through her at Mark Fisher's oily tones. 'How are you settling in? Everything to your … liking?'

Gem bit down on the inside of her cheek to resist telling her boss that she'd rather be stuck in the middle of nowhere at the Green Man, than within one hundred miles of him. 'Dan and I are settling in just fine, thank you. Already starting to feel like home.'

There was a snort on the other end of the phone. 'Well, any time you feel like coming back to civilisation, I'm sure we can come to an agreement. For a price.'

A price that would be paid flat on her back, Gem knew. 'That won't be necessary, thank you, Mr Fisher. We're perfectly happy right where we are. Together.' She hung up the phone before he could respond, and slumped against the bar, sheet slipping down around her shoulders.

'Who was that?' Dan asked from behind her, and Gem turned to see him leaning against the doorway from the flat upstairs, wearing only his boxer shorts. His arms were crossed over his muscled chest, and his face was dark.

No point lying, Gem knew. Who else would be calling them on the pub number, anyway? 'Mark Fisher.'

Dan's arms unfolded and he stepped forward, the movement almost predatory, a big cat waiting to strike. 'Really. And what did our illustrious boss have to say?'

'Just checking how we were settling in.' Gem swallowed as her husband took another step towards her, reaching out to run a finger along the line of the sheet where it cut across the top of her breast.

'Was that all?'

What had he heard? What had he guessed? Gem couldn't concentrate on her story with Dan's searing touch running across her overheated flesh. 'That was all.'

'Nothing about why we've been exiled to this place?' His finger was under the sheet now, making its lazy way down between her breasts.

'No.' It was sort of true. The conversation had been more about what she'd need to do to get them *out* of exile.

'Shame.' Dan pulled on the sheet, tugging her towards him, his arm wrapping around her waist as Gem found her cheek nuzzled up against the hard muscles of his torso. 'But if there's one good thing about being in the middle of nowhere, it's that you're miles away from him. I hated the way he looked at you.'

'I know. I hated it too.' Gem blinked as her eyes were drawn to the window again, sparkling in the sunshine. She had hated it, when Mark Fisher looked at her. But last night …

Dan's hands wandered up over her curves, untucking the sheet from under her arms. 'Maybe there is one other good thing,' he murmured against her ear, as the fabric pooled around her feet. 'Nobody to watch me do this.'

As he picked up her naked body, carrying her up the stairs to dump her back in bed, Gem ignored the very small part of her mind that whispered, *Shame.*

She was happy with Dan. She loved Dan. And he would always be more than enough for her.

She just had to keep reminding herself of that.

By midday, the heat was unbearable.

Gem had thrown on her lightest sun dress in the hope of staying cool, even though it was too nice to waste on cleaning the pub. But as she clambered on top of another table to reach the top panes of another window, cleaning spray and cloths in hand, she could still feel the sweat trickling down her back.

Every muscle ached; a combination of rigorous cleaning and enthusiastic sex. With the added lack of sleep, Gem was about ready to drop.

Sweeping her cloth across the glass, Gem reached out with her other hand to grab the window frame for balance, and felt her fingers knock against something on the wall. She groaned as she heard wood hit wood, and dropped her cloth onto the windowsill as she climbed down from the table to see what she'd knocked off.

The walls of the pub were covered in trinkets and knick knacks and pictures, some hung in groups and themes, but more often they were displayed with no discernable logic at all. Dan would want to take them down eventually, she was sure. Not his style. If they stayed at the Green Man long enough, they'd want to make it their own. Redecorate properly, maybe. But the walls underneath were uneven, and desperately in need of painting, so for now the clutter remained.

Her bare feet hit the wooden floorboards, and she bent down, groping blindly under the table for the object. Her hands brushed against wood, and she wrapped her fingers around whatever it was, pulling it out into the light.

Sitting back on her heels, she examined it. The mask, again, she realised. The one she'd spotted the night before that had so dramatically affected her mood. Except, of course, it was just a carving. It couldn't affect her at all. Pure coincidence, surely.

Still, she had to admit to a little curiosity.

Pushing herself up, she perched on the edge of a nearby chair, laying the mask on the table in front of her. It seemed undamaged, at least. The warm wood leaves still curled around that wide forehead, those deep, deep eyes. Strange how the artist had got such depth, such feeling into the eyes, when really, they were each nothing but a circle of wood.

Still, she was glad she hadn't broken it. The vines twisting over the high cheekbones, the curve of the mouth, almost mocking, but still soft. Seductive.

Gem swallowed, suddenly aware of a hot feeling caused by more than just the oppressive weather, coursing through her body. This heat didn't tire her, didn't make her want to collapse and do nothing for the rest of the day.

This heat made her *want*.

Running a finger across the wooden lips of the mask, Gem felt an unnatural warmth coming from the wood. *Sunlight,* she told herself. The sun must have warmed it. Except the spot where it usually sat on the wall was in shade.

Enough of this. It was crazy, thinking that a mask had any powers at all. Shoving her chair back, Gem picked up the mask and hung it back on the wall, where it could just stop bothering her, thank you.

Grabbing her cloth again, she went to clean a window on the other side of the pub. Far away from the mask. But her body wouldn't let her forget it.

Her nipples were hard under her dress, she realised. So hard that they ached, desperate for touch, for a mouth around them. Her thigh muscles longed to stretch and spread, ready for a hard cock between them. And her knickers, God, they were soaked through …

The door to the pub banged open, and she spun round to face it.

'OK, that's it,' Dan said, hauling the last crate of bottles inside and dumping it next to the fridges. 'I'm calling a halt. I think, siesta, then we'll start up again when it cools down.'

Gem looked at him, sweat stained and gorgeous, panting a little as he leant against the bar. Her body tightened further, and she couldn't help but think of him upstairs in their bed again. It had been good, so good that morning. Even if she hadn't quite managed not to think about the door opening, and her watcher from the night before walking in … *Focus, Gem.*

'Do you think we'll be ready for tomorrow night?' she

93

asked, desperate for distraction. Her body was betraying her, taking her mind away from her husband, wanting more than one pair of hands on her skin. Could it really be the mask, making her want these things? Her eyes couldn't stay away from the window, looking out over the bridge. She blinked. Was there someone standing there? A figure, dark and shadowed under the trees. Was it *him?*

'I think we have to be,' Dan said. He stretched his arms up above his head and yawned. 'Announcement's gone out. I think Mark Bloody Fisher even put it in the paper. If there's anyone living around here beyond woodland creatures, I'll bet you they'll be here for the beer tomorrow night.' He gave her a crooked smile. 'But that doesn't mean we haven't got time to take a break until it's cool enough to breathe down here.'

Gem tried to smile back but it felt weak and tired on her lips. 'You go on up. I've got to get some fresh air.' She glanced back at the window; there was no one on the bridge now, even if there ever had been. 'Maybe I'll see if the woods are any cooler.' She had to get away from this pub, from that mask. From these feelings.

Dan nodded, smothering another yawn. 'Well, you know where I'll be,' he said, blowing her a kiss before climbing the stairs to their bedroom.

Gem watched him go, wondering what she was doing, what she even thought would happen. There wouldn't be anyone out there, of course there wouldn't. And it wasn't like she'd set out to seduce them if there were.

No. She just needed to get out of the heat; that was all. She couldn't think straight, with the muggy air closing in on her. A cool, river breeze, and she'd feel more like herself again, she was sure.

Something had to shake these strange longings that were hanging around her. And she was running out of other ideas.

Chapter Three

THE WOODS WERE BLISSFULLY shady. For the first time since they arrived at the Green Man, Gem felt like she could breathe again. She sucked in the sweet, clear air, and felt the cool breeze through the trees drying the sheen of sweat on her skin. The thin cotton of her sun dress swirled around her legs, rather than clinging to her, and Gem felt the weight of the last few days lifting from her shoulders.

She followed the path from the bridge, away from the river and deep into the heart of the woods. But the stream obviously twisted back on itself because, after 20 minutes of walking away from it, Gem heard the babbling of water over stones, and stepped instinctively towards it.

Her breath caught in her throat as she looked out over the most perfect glade she could imagine. The trees thinned out there, revealing the stream, more of a brook at this point, bubbling and dancing through the centre, edged by lush, dewy grass on either bank. Overhead, the sky was still as blue, the sun still as bright, but the oppressive heat that had swallowed the county for days was gone.

But it was still more than warm enough for a paddle …

Slipping her feet out of her sandals, Gem slid down to the edge of the riverbank, dangling her feet down into the cool, cool river. Her eyes fluttered closed as she leant back on her elbows, her breaths evening out as her body relaxed, muscle by muscle, breath by breath. How could she worry in a place as perfect as this?

She could forget about Mark Fisher, forget about her watcher, forget about the mask, forget all her wants and dark desires …

For a moment, she was utterly carefree.

Then, between one breath and the next, something changed. Her body realised it before her mind, and her eyes flew open. The glade looked as it had before, but the sun seemed a little brighter, the grass a little greener. And the sounds of the woods were muted, the stream almost silent, as if she were locked away in a separate bubble of time.

She leant back further, eyes searching the glade behind her, and gasped. There, stepping between the trees, towards her, was the most beautiful man she'd ever seen. An unreal, inhuman sort of beautiful. Unbelievable.

I'm dreaming, she realised, and felt her growing tension ebb away again. Of course it was a dream. No man looked that perfect.

His chestnut hair curled around his face, falling almost into eyes Gem knew, even from a distance, were a deep forest green. His white shirt was open and loose at the neck, showing hints of the tanned and muscled torso underneath. A curling, twining tattoo of what looked like oak leaves started at his heart and curved up over one broad shoulder. Sensual lips parted in a smile, and Gem swallowed hard, knowing with certainty, in a way she only ever did in dreams, that this was the man who had watched her make love to her husband the night before.

The man she'd imagined joining them.

'I saw you,' he said, and his voice brushed past her like the wind through the leaves. 'Last night.'

Gem sat up as he moved closer, walking barefoot through the grass towards her. 'You were on the bridge,' she managed, as he sat down close beside her, the crisp coolness of his shirt rasping against her skin. 'You … you watched us.'

The man nodded, no shame in his eyes, only heat. 'I did. You were beautiful.'

A blush, starting in her cheeks and running right down

96

over her chest, heated Gem's skin. Just as well it was a dream, or she'd be horribly embarrassed. Not just at the pink flush staining her skin, but the way her nipples had tightened at the sound of the stranger's voice. They were hard and heavy under her bra and she knew, without even looking down, that he had to be able to see them through the thin cotton of her dress.

'I imagined ...' her voice trailed off. Even in a dream, she couldn't bring herself to articulate what she'd wanted.

'You fantasised about me joining you, didn't you?' His voice was soft, as gentle as his fingers as they reached out to trace the side of her face. Gem bit her lip, and nodded, her heart skipping faster at his touch. Then he leant closer, his hair brushing against her shoulder, and whispered close in her ear, 'So did I.'

Too much, Gem's body screamed, even as it bent into him, without any instruction from her mind. The breath of warm air in her ear sent shivers straight through her. Every inch of her skin craved his touch, her lips begged to feel his against them, her hair wanted his fingers tangled in it, and further down, between her legs, she throbbed for the feel of him.

'What ...' she tried to say, but her mouth was dry and her voice came out husky. She licked her lips and tried again. 'What did you imagine doing?'

The smile that spread across his too perfect face was predatory, hungry. His body slid behind her, his hands running over her shoulders, her spine as he moved. He straddled her body, one leg either side of her hips, pulling her back against his hard chest. Gem wondered if he could feel her heart racing under the arm that wrapped around her.

'I watched as you bared your breasts,' he said, his voice warm in her ear, resonating through her bones. 'I wanted to touch them, hold them, feel them heavy in my hands.'

Her breasts were aching for touch now. Had been ever since she looked at the mask that morning. 'Please,' Gem said, the words wrenched from her throat.

A low chuckle behind her, and Gem felt one hand reaching up to untie the straps of her dress, the fabric falling down to her waist. Her bra followed right behind, and suddenly Gem was topless, the breeze making her nipples tighten further. 'Please,' she said again, desperate now, and his hands came up to cup her breasts, the smooth skin of his palms heavenly against her nipples.

'So firm,' he murmured over her shoulder. 'So heavy and warm and wanting. I dreamt about holding them like this, of stroking my fingers over them like this.' He spread his hands out across the span of each breast, leaving the rosy tips of her nipples poking between his fingers. Then he squeezed his fingers together, and the exquisite pressure made Gem gasp. It felt exactly as she had imagined, which made sense she supposed, in the tiny remote part of her brain that was still working. This was her dream, after all.

'I watched as your husband licked his way inside you.' As he said it, Gem felt a familiar pressure between her legs, that wonderful swirl around her clit that Dan knew drove her wild. As if he were really there, re-enacting the night before as her dream man described it. 'And I watched as he laid you on the table and thrust into you.'

A jolt flew through Gem's body, a sudden, sharp burst of pleasure. Her head tipped back as she took stock of her body; dream man's hands were still firmly on her breasts, but she could feel herself being filled by a beautifully hard cock. She looked down, almost expecting to see Dan between her legs pressing into her, but there was nobody there.

'What then?' she gasped. 'What did you want to do then?'

But she already knew, of course, even as her dream man's fingers started trailing down over her stomach. Because it was just what she'd done, what she'd wished for, lying there spread open on the table.

'I wanted to reach down to where you were joined,' he said, his fingers brushing through her curls and parting her. 'I wanted to touch you, right here.' One finger, hard against her clit, enough to send wonderful shudders through her middle. 'I wanted to bring you higher and higher, even as your husband fucked you into the table.'

Competing sensations flooded Gem's body. The rhythmic filling of her body that she knew could only be in her mind, against the twist and brush of fingers on her clit, just the way she'd done it herself the night before. And then there was her dream man, leaning around her shoulder to take a nipple in his mouth, drawing a moan from her throat.

His mouth should have been hot, but just as she'd imagined, every part of his touch was cold, a blissful coolness against her overheating body. And just as she had spread out on that table, Gem felt her body thrumming harder, tension rising, stretching and stretching until …

She broke, shuddering under his hands, his mouth, shaking at the intensity. Breath coming in pants, her eyes squeezed shut as aftershocks ran through her body. She heard her dream man chuckle softly next to her ear, before lying her down on the dewy grass, her dress still tangled around her waist, her underwear missing.

Long moments later, Gem found the energy to open her eyes again, and when she looked, the glade had returned to normal, and her dream man was gone. I'm awake, she thought, sitting up, and knew it must be true.

But she was still half naked on the grass.

When Dan woke from his siesta, Gem still hadn't returned. Shifting under the thin sheets, Dan ran a hand down his chest towards his half hard cock, imagining Gem crawling into bed with him, making her way under the sheets …

His body hardened further as he built the image up in his mind. She'd stand beside the bed for a moment, watching him as he lazily stroked his cock. Dan reached down and wrapped a hand around himself, eyes slitted as he imagined watching Gem, watching him.

She'd bite her lip, he thought, in that adorably hot way she had, when she wanted to do something, but hadn't quite decided to yet. Then, decision made, she'd reach up and unfasten the ties of that sun dress that had been driving him crazy all morning.

Dan's eyes closed completely, as he gave himself over to the daydream.

The fabric would pool at her feet, leaving her naked underneath, he decided, and his hand tightened involuntarily around his cock at the mental vision. She'd step closer, towards the bed, placing her hands on the sheets, either side of his legs. Then first one knee, then the other, as she crawled up the mattress towards him, her beautiful breasts swaying in time with her hips as she moved, hypnotising him. Her eyes, wide and bright and mischievous as her hands pulled the sheet down, away from his hot, sticky body. God, he could just see it …

She wouldn't waste time, he decided. Just run her hands down his chest before gripping his straining cock in her hands, licking her lips at the sight of him. She'd run her tongue around him, like she always did, knowing it drove him crazy. Then she'd swallow him down as he watched, her bottom in the air as she worked, leaving her pussy invitingly open. And maybe, just maybe, there'd be someone there to take advantage of it, while he watched …

Dan's eyes flew open, his hand jerking away from his aching hard cock.

No. No, no no. God no!

Why would he want that? Of course he didn't want that. Who would want to watch another man fuck his wife?

No. Absolutely not.

Downstairs, a door slammed, and Dan sat up, arousal fading. It must be the heat, he decided. It was getting to him. He couldn't think straight. That was what it was.

God, they needed to get away from this godforsaken pub. Maybe Mark Fisher could find them something in Scotland. It was colder in Scotland, right? Worth a try, anyway.

Tugging on his jeans, Dan padded down the stairs, T-shirt still in hand. Too bloody hot for any unnecessary clothing. He paused at the entrance to the bar, watching Gem as she attacked the already swept floor with her brush again. Guess the woods weren't as calming as she hoped.

'Did you have a nice walk?' he asked, and Gem dropped the broom. He stepped forward to pick it up for her, pretending not to notice the way she skittered back from him. Or the fact she had leaves in her hair.

'It was fine,' she said, grabbing the brush from his hands.

'Cooler in the woods?'

Gem started sweeping again, with even greater force. Gonna be no floorboards left, at this rate. 'A little.'

'Maybe I'll take a walk myself, later.' Dan watched as his wife froze, just for a second, in her sweeping endeavours.

'You've already had a siesta,' she said, turning away from him. 'Don't you think we'd better get some work done before you slack off any more?'

At the memory of his siesta, and his daydream, Dan stepped back, away from his beautiful wife, who never needed to know the terrible things he let himself think, sometimes. 'You're right,' he said, moving behind the bar, towards the stairs to the cellar. 'I'll just start stocking the fridges then, shall I?'

He could still hear the bristles of the brush scraping against the wood of the floorboards as he descended the stairs towards the crates of bottled beer. There was definitely something going on with Gem, he thought, and felt something hot and furious rising through his body. Whatever it was, Dan was willing to bet it had something to do with Mark Bloody Fisher.

Now he just had to find out what.

Chapter Four

THE GREEN MAN PUB threw open its doors again the following night and, to Gem and Dan's amazement, customers poured in. Glad of the distraction, Gem smiled and flirted and served and chatted with every person who visited. But, somewhere at the back of her mind where she couldn't quite admit the truth to herself, she knew that she was waiting for just one person.

He didn't come.

Had he been a dream? Gem hoped so. The idea that she might have cheated on her husband without even knowing it made her burn with shame. But the idea that her dream man might be real …

No. She had to stop thinking like that. Even if he *was* real, what did it matter? She didn't want him without Dan, and Dan would never, ever share her. No point even considering it.

Instead, Gem threw herself into her work, whirling around the tables collecting empty glasses, while Dan pulled pints and measured spirits behind the bar. He looked at home there, Gem realised, pausing for a moment beside a window table. Maybe more at home than he had in years, even at the Eagle. Something about the rustic beams over his dark head, the easy smile for the locals, the comfortable conversation. Despite all his objections, Dan belonged in a place like the Green Man. With loyal locals, instead of raucous, drunken 20-somethings, looking for the next cool hang out. He was more himself, here.

Gem sighed. If only she could say the same for herself.

Seemed to her, she'd been a whole new person, ever since they arrived.

'Now, that's far too sad a sigh for such a happy occasion.' Gemma looked down at the words, to see a smiling, elderly gentleman watching her over his pint. 'Whatever can be making you so melancholy?'

Gem shook her head. 'I'm not sad. Just …'

'Wistful?'

That sounded about right. Wistful, wishing for something that could never be. 'Maybe.'

The man gestured towards the empty seat opposite him. 'Why not rest your feet for a moment and tell me about it?'

Gem bit the inside of her cheek. No way in hell was she telling anyone about her latest fantasies, let alone some random old man in the pub.

He chuckled. 'Well, why not sit down and keep me company for a minute, anyway. I've been watching you tonight. You haven't stopped for a moment.'

That much was true. In her efforts to distract herself, Gem had been working at double speed all evening. 'Maybe just for a moment.'

She sank into the blissfully padded chair, realising suddenly how much her legs ached. But the pain faded as something else caught her attention, and she realised exactly which window table she was sitting at. To her left, a face stared at her; the carved wood face of the Green Man, oak leaves covering his cheeks and forehead, leaving only his eyes uncovered. *That bloody mask again.* But she could swear she had seen those eyes in a human face …

'Our very own Green Man,' her companion said, gesturing to the carving. 'Do you know much about him?'

Gem shook her head, still staring at the unblinking eyes of the carving. They were unpainted, warm brown circles under delicately rendered lids. But she couldn't help thinking that they ought to be green. She could feel them watching her, could imagine those lips quirking up into an amused smile. She bit her lip as she realised her nipples had tightened again at the thought. God, this was ridiculous! She was a grown woman. She had to have better control over her body than this, surely.

'He shows up all over Europe, you know.' Gem tore her eyes away from the carving to pay attention to the old man's words. Distraction. That was what she needed. To forget all about the stupid mask, and fantasy men in wooded groves. 'In churches, on buildings, pubs, fountains. Everywhere. Some say he's Bacchus, or Dionysus. Some that he's a tree god. Or the King of May, or Jack in the Green, or even the Summer Lord. But no one really knows for sure.'

'What does he mean?' Gem asked, gaze trailing back to the carving. Its wooden eyes burnt into her skin, as if to say, *I know your dreams*. She looked away again, towards Dan at the bar. He was her only dream. 'I mean, I assume he's a symbol of something?'

The man didn't answer immediately, and when Gem turned back to him, an apologetic smile on her lips, she found him watching her, an assessing look on his face. Finally, he said, 'The Green Man means many things to many people. To some, he's a promise of summer after winter. For some, a rebalancing of nature. For some a fertility spirit. Maybe all three.'

A god of sex and summer and nature. Gem's teeth bit into her lip as her afternoon in the woods replayed in her mind once more. Those green eyes, so like those in the carving. The twisting, twining oak leaf tattoo over his heart, running up over that muscled shoulder. The ridiculous response her body had to that mask, every single time.

It was impossible, of course. But what if it wasn't? What if she'd truly met an incarnation of the Green Man – and been seduced by him?

One advantage of being out in the sticks, Gem decided, was that the locals were used to last call being at eleven, and they were all toddling home well before midnight. Dan locked up behind the last of them and turned back to face her, leaning against the heavy wood door.

'Not bad, for a first night,' he said, rubbing a hand across his eyes. He looked frazzled, his hair mussed from running his hands through it, and there were splashes of beer across his shirt.

Frazzled, but gorgeous. Gem stepped out from behind the bar, towards him, hands itching to smooth down his hair, then run across his shoulders, digging into the muscles there until they relaxed. 'And you thought there'd be nobody here but woodland creatures.'

Wrapping one arm around his waist, she led Dan to the chair at the window table, and pressed down on his shoulders until he sank into it with a groan.

'God, I feel like I haven't sat down for days. I never felt like this after a shift at the Eagle,' Dan said.

Gem moved behind him, hands kneading across his shoulders, enjoying the bunch and release of his muscles under her fingers. 'You haven't got any pretty little bar girls and boys to help you here,' she pointed out, remembering the flock of college students they'd hired to keep the three bars of the Eagle flowing freely.

Dan tipped his head back and smiled at her. 'Why would I need them? I have you.'

'Oh, that's very nice.' The words came out almost as a purr, and Gem let her hands slide forward, over her husband's shoulders and down the hard planes of his chest. Her mouth up against his ear, she popped the first button through its hole, and whispered, 'Maybe you deserve a little treat. For all your hard work.'

Turning his head, Dan caught her lips with his, and Gem's fingers fumbled on the next button at the heat of his mouth. 'A treat?' he murmured, pulling away.

Gem slid around the chair, dropping to her knees between his legs. God, she loved him like this. Playful and wanting and waiting for her … She reached up and tugged open the last few buttons, pushing back the fabric of his shirt so she could run her hands across his chest, down his stomach, trailing through the hair that led down under his jeans.

'Well,' she said. 'You have been very good.' She flicked open the buttons of his jeans, and heard him groan.

'I have.' Dan's head dropped into a nod, and Gem looked up into his warm, brown eyes. *Not green,* she reminded herself. 'I really have.'

Resting her hands on his thighs, Gem leant forward, her hair brushing against Dan's stomach before her lips did. She breathed in the spicy, hot scent of him, placing kisses along his skin, moving inexorably lower and lower. She could feel his whole torso rising and falling as his breaths grew deeper, and she smiled against him. Right now, she knew, right at this second, before she took him in her mouth but after he knew she was going to, right at that moment, she could ask him for anything and get it.

I could ask for my dream man to join us …

But she wouldn't. Not just because – *come on Gemma!* – he didn't exist. But because once the idea was out there, she could never take it back. And while Dan might agree to anything if it meant he'd feel her lips wrapped around him, once the heat of the moment had passed … She didn't want to learn how he'd look at her when he realised what she really wanted.

Enough. Dan's breath was hot and desperate against the top of her head, his hands clutching against her shoulders. She'd tortured him long enough. Dipping her head lower, she brushed her lips against his straining cock, and felt his hips jolt up to meet her. 'Easy there,' she murmured, her words vibrating against his hardness.

'God, Gem, please, just …'

Gem allowed herself a smug smile before she licked her way up the length of him. Almost incoherent already. She *was* good.

Before he could find any words, she slipped her mouth over the bulging head, her tongue swirling round. She loved the feel of him, hot and heavy in her mouth. The softness of his skin under her tongue. The groan she drew up from deep inside his chest when she gripped him tight at the base with one hand, then sucked him in as far as she could go. She felt powerful, like this. In control.

At least, usually.

Something felt different tonight. Gem raised her eyes, as far as she could without releasing Dan, looking for what had changed. There, up on the wall. The Green Man. Gem blinked. That was impossible.

Instead of the wooden eyes she knew were set into the carving's face, she would swear that green irises were staring down at her. Watching her.

Gem closed her eyes, turning her full attention back to her husband, squeezing his cock a little with her left hand. Dan groaned appreciatively.

But she was too late to stop the fantasy, already rising up in her mind.

What if he was out there, again, her dream man, whoever he was? What if he was watching, right now, as she made love to her husband's cock with her mouth? What if …

Ghostly hands brushed against Gem's hips, and she pulled her mouth off Dan with a gasp.

'What?' Dan asked, his voice muzzy with lust. 'Gem?'

Swallowing, she glanced back over her shoulder, not knowing quite what she expected to see. But there was no one there. 'It's fine, love,' she murmured, moving her mouth back over him. *God, am I so desperate that I've started hallucinating a third person in our sex life?*

Even as she thought it, she felt those impossible hands on her again, running from her hips up to her waist, and back down again. Gem's hand tightened around Dan, and she heard him gasp above her. But she could barely concentrate on him. Not when …

Oh God. Her hallucination was lifting her now, tugging her up on to her knees. Gem rested her arms across Dan's thighs for balance, peeking up at him through her lashes. Her husband's head was thrown back against the chair, his body slumped down, giving in to the sensations her mouth was drawing out in him. Even if there was anything to see, going on behind her, he'd never notice.

A hot, wicked thrill ran through Gem's body at the thought. It might only be imaginary, but those hands on her waist felt real enough. Even as they ran down her thighs, then pushed her skirt up, bunching it around her waist. God, they felt very real indeed.

Her body obviously believed in them, Gem thought, as she realised her knickers were soaked through. As much as she loved going down on her husband, it didn't usually produce such an extreme response. She was dripping wet, aching for touch, her skin crackling with need. Normally, she'd snake one hand down between her thighs, bringing herself off while she worked Dan over. But tonight ...

One imaginary hand released her hip, leaving Gem bereft for a moment, until she felt it brushing against her inner thigh, higher and higher until it reached the drenched fabric of her knickers. Her breath caught in her throat as she felt the fabric pushed aside, felt the warm night air against her wetness, and the hard, hot, tip of a cock pressing against her entrance.

'Gem?' Dan's voice above her made her realise she'd stopped moving. Quickly, she sank her mouth back down over him, taking him in as far as he'd go, before slowly lifting back up again. But even as she repeated the movement again and again, her attention was on the pressure at her centre, steady and still. What was he waiting for? If he was her hallucination, her fantasy, shouldn't he just ...

There. Before she could finish the thought, her dream man plunged into her, filling her up so completely that she moaned around Dan's cock, and heard him chuckle.

'Touching yourself, love?' he asked, smiling down at her with half closed eyes. 'Wondered how long you'd hold out.'

But she wasn't. This was so much better.

Her imaginary man was thrusting into her now, steady firm strokes that pushed her mouth down hard over Dan, then pulled her back again, setting up a rhythm she had no choice but to follow. Dan groaned at the sudden increase in pace, and Gem felt her whole body vibrate with the sound. This, this was what she'd needed all along. To be here, caught between two men, each fucking her in their way. Knowing they both needed her, wanted her. This was more than desire. This was desperation and urgency, and it felt wonderful.

If only it were real ...

But she couldn't dwell on that now. Not with the rising hum in her blood, and the way her muscles were starting to tense and release. Not with the spiralling sensation of urgency under her skin. Not when she was *so fucking close ...*

Her grip tightened around the base of Dan's cock, making him groan, as she swallowed him a little bit deeper. Behind her, her dream lover was picking up speed, growing closer and closer, just as she was. *Now, now, now,* her mind chanted, desperation filling her, coiling in her middle so tightly she knew she'd scream if it didn't break soon.

A moan escaped from her lips, and the very feel of it was enough to send Dan over the edge. His hips hitched up, pushing his cock deeper down her throat as he came, and Gem swallowed reflexively, even as the imaginary hands on her hips gripped tighter, hard enough that she almost believed she might have bruises the next day. Then he dove into her, further than he had so far, deeper than Gem had thought possible, and every cell in her body broke apart and she screamed as she came, harder than she ever had before.

'Glad you enjoyed that, too,' Dan said, one hand stroking her hair as she rested her cheek against the hard muscle of his thigh. 'Maybe I can return the favour again tomorrow.'

Gem sat back on her heels, knowing her dream lover was long gone, if he'd ever been there at all, as more than a figment of her overactive imagination. And even though her heart still pounded, her blood still pulsed in her temples as she struggled to even out her breathing. Even though the aftershocks of her orgasm were still echoing through her body …

She couldn't help but imagine Dan's tongue on her, while her dream lover fucked her again.

Chapter Five

GEMMA'S DAYS AT THE Green Man settled into a comfortable routine almost before she realised it. They opened at eleven thirty, usually to find a couple of older men already outside, waiting for their first pint of the day. They served bar snacks and drinks to a small but steady stream of walkers, locals and cyclists throughout the afternoon, before business picked up around teatime. They called time at eleven, packed up, fell into bed exhausted and woke up late the next day, ready to start again.

The weather didn't break, despite the forecasts; if anything, it grew hotter, stickier, and more unbearable. By the Friday of their first full week there, after a morning of snapping at each other over tiny things, Gem reached breaking point.

'I'm going for a walk,' she said, tossing a damp bar cloth over the back of one of the stools that lined the length of the serving area.

'Now?' Dan glanced up from where he was cooling his head inside one of the fridges.

'I need some air.' Gem waved an arm around the practically empty bar. The old man she'd spoken to the other night was ensconced at his usual window table, but otherwise the place was empty. 'We've had one customer all morning. It's too hot for anyone else to trek out here today. You'll be OK on your own for half an hour.'

Dan looked as if he wanted to say something more, his brow creasing into a frown as he got to his feet. But Gem wasn't in the mood to argue, or even discuss. Turning on her heel, she stepped towards the entrance, feeling her shoulders lift as the door slammed shut behind her.

The woods were blissfully cool, and Gem picked up her pace, the breeze at her back hurrying her along. She wanted to be in her glade, feet in the river, icy water rushing around her ankles.

She wanted to see if *he* would be there again.

The pub had been too hot, too busy, too demanding, for sex, since the night in the bar. But that didn't mean the thrumming in her veins had died down, the vague feeling of need that had haunted her since their arrival. She wasn't herself, she knew that. But she couldn't dislike the person she was, the person who felt so much, wanted so much.

Still, at the back of her mind, a nagging thought had persisted all week, pushing its way forward until she couldn't ignore it any more.

If this new her was real ... what if her dream man was too?

She needed to find out, before the question drove her crazy. So, pulling at the front of her blouse to let the air hit her skin, Gem stepped into the glade and looked around.

For a moment, it seemed like the clearing was empty. The only noises were the rushing water of the stream, the only scent that of fresh, green leaves. But there was something ... a feeling, a sense not covered by the usual five. Gem knew she wasn't alone.

The grass sprung underfoot as Gem moved into the centre and turned slowly around, studying the trees. Leaves and branches swayed and moved in the breeze, sending shadows skittering across the tree trunks until the whole forest seemed to be shifting. But, when she looked closely ... She stopped, standing staring at the biggest oak tree edging the glade.

'I see you,' she lied. It wasn't sight, so much. More a feeling, intuition. He was there, she could feel him.

A chuckle, low and deep, came from the tree. Then, the

leaves shifted again and he stood there before her, his tanned skin glowing bronze in the sunlight. No shirt, this time, just dark brown trousers that clung to his muscled thighs. And there, coiling up from his heart over his shoulder, was the tattoo she remembered, the pattern suddenly more familiar. Those oak leaves and acorns, the twist of the stems. She knew now where she'd seen them before. They were painted on her pub sign. They were carved into the face of the Green Man on the pub wall.

She raised her eyes to meet his gaze. The green eyes that looked back at her were familiar, too. Had she imagined them, staring at her from the Green Man mask?

'You have questions,' he said, a smirk playing around his lips.

Gem's head jerked up and down, the motion stiff, as if she'd lost all control of her own body. 'I do.'

'Then ask them.'

There were so many, Gem knew. So much she needed to ask. But the words that came to her lips were, 'Are you real?'

Definitely a smirk now. 'Depends on your definition of reality.'

That wasn't an answer, Gem knew. But if he wasn't entirely real, he must be partly fantasy. And a fantasy wasn't cheating, was it?

'What's your name?'

He chuckled again, and Gem could almost feel the sound, travelling through the ground at their feet, up into her chest. 'I have many names. The Lord of Summer. The Green Man.' He stepped forward, closer, close enough to run a finger down the side of her neck. Gem shivered. 'You may call me Jack.'

'Jack,' she echoed, as his finger travelled lower, tracing a line between her breasts.

'That's right.' He popped the first button on her shirt. 'Do you have other questions?'

'I … I can't remember.'

Another button fell away, her shirt gaping open now, revealing the white lace of her bra beneath. 'Then maybe I should ask one.'

'OK,' Gem managed, as the last button popped and Jack brought both hands up to push the shirt away from her shoulders, down onto the grass below.

He leant in close, breath warm and sweet against her face. 'What do you want me to do to you?'

Finally, Gem thought. *A question she knew the answer to.*

'I want the whole fantasy.' Her skin tingled under his gaze, the heat in his green eyes making her heart beat faster. 'I want you inside me.'

Jack stepped closer still, his body pressing up tight against hers. 'That's not all you want though, is it?'

Gem swallowed. 'No. I want my husband to see it. I want him to want it too. I want him to join us.'

Dipping his head, Jack kissed the base of her neck, just where it joined her shoulder. 'I can't make promises for others. But the first part … that at least I can give you.'

There should have been more guilt, Gem reflected briefly, as Jack's hands stripped her bra from her body and freed her breasts, lowering his mouth to suckle at one tight, hard nipple. But if Jack was a fantasy, how could she feel guilt about how wonderful it felt to have his mouth on her?

Then Jack's hands were stripping away her skirt, his fingers tracing up the inside of her thighs, closer and closer to where she needed them, and Gem couldn't think about anything, any more.

It wasn't that Dan blamed Gem for needing a break. God only knew, the constantly rising temperature and lack of air conditioning in the pub would drive anyone mad. And yes, OK, so he'd been a little short with her that morning. Not that she hadn't been just as snappy, mind you. Still, overall, he'd much rather she walk her bad mood out of her system

114

than have her yelling at him for the rest of the day.

It was just that he couldn't shake the feeling that he was missing something.

Mopping the sweat from his forehead with a clean bar cloth, Dan leant against the bar and tried to put his finger on exactly what had seemed wrong, or unusual. It was just so hard to think in this heat …

'Where do you think she's gone?' The voice, creaky and old, surprised Dan into standing up straight again. He glanced around the bar until he caught the amused eyes of the elderly gentleman sitting by the door. 'Your wife,' the man clarified, as if Dan couldn't have guessed who he was talking about. 'The one that just ran out of here like a teenager late for her first date.'

And there it was. The truth of what he'd been missing hit Dan in the gut, and he grabbed hold of the edge of the bar for stability. It wasn't that Gem had seemed eager to get out of the pub. It was that she'd seemed like *she had somewhere else she'd rather be.*

'I don't know,' Dan said, the horror of it rising in him, making his muscles tremble. 'I don't know where she is.'

Could it be Mark Fisher? What if he was in town? What if that was why he'd called Gem earlier in the week? What if they'd arranged to meet somewhere?

Oh God, anyone *but Mark Bloody Fisher. Please, Gem.*

But who else could it be, really? They'd been there a week. When had she had time to meet anyone else?

'You all right, son?' the man by the door asked, and Dan forced a stiff nod.

'Fine. I'm just …' The phone rang, saving him from trying to find the words for exactly what he was. 'The Green Man Pub,' he said, picking it up.

'Daniel.' For the first time, Mark Fisher's voice oozing down the phone line didn't make Dan want to hit something. Because if Mark was calling here, that meant he wasn't out seducing Gem. Didn't it? He could hear the familiar sounds of a busy pub at lunchtime in the background; clinking cutlery, glasses hitting wood, the quiz machine … Nowhere Gem could have reached on foot sounded like that. 'Is your wife there?'

Dan felt a cautious hope somewhere in his chest. 'She's gone out for a walk. Won't I do?'

'Not for my needs.' How did he put so much innuendo into four words?

'She's not interested in your needs,' Dan said, his voice sharp. 'I've already told you that.'

Even Fisher's laugh was greasy. 'I'll have to hear that from her own lips, if you don't mind. We've been discussing an … agreement. One that you have no part in.'

Something tightened in his throat, and for a moment Dan thought he might choke on the words. 'Gem would never …' he trailed off. Wasn't that what he'd just been contemplating?

'Wouldn't she?' Mark chuckled, a dark, horrible sound. 'Did she tell you about her and me in the beer cellar? Did she tell you how she –'

Dan hung up.

Pushing the conversation from his mind, he tried to focus. He couldn't trust that oily bastard over his own wife. But still … OK, so Gem wasn't with Mark Fisher. But there was definitely something going on with her. And Dan thought it was about time he found out what.

'Everything OK?' The old guy had his eyebrows raised, but he didn't look concerned, Dan realised. More as if he were watching a film, one where he already knew the ending.

Dan shook his head. No time to wonder at the peculiarities of his customer base. 'I need to go and find my wife,' he said, throwing his towel onto the bar. 'Can you keep an eye on things here?'

'Not like I have anywhere else to be,' the man said, with a shrug of his bony shoulders. 'And if I were you, I'd try the woods first.'

'Thanks,' Dan said, and headed for the bridge.

Chapter Six

THE WOODS WERE ANOTHER world, and Dan couldn't think for the life of him why he hadn't explored them before, in the last week. The haze of confusion and bitterness that had clouded his head since they arrived lifted the moment he stepped off the bridge and into the cool, leafy shade of the trees. The oppressive heat no longer clouded his ability to reason, and the relief of feeling in his right mind again was all consuming.

And as the rustling breeze hit his overheated skin, Dan realised he wasn't mad at Gemma for walking out. He wasn't even mad at Mark Fisher, the oily bastard. He knew exactly what had made him angry, had known it for a long time. He was mad at himself. At his own desires and needs.

He paused in the shade of an ancient oak tree, the rough bark scratching his back through his thin summer shirt as he leant against it. Letting out a breath, he finally allowed the thought he'd been blocking for so long enter his mind freely.

It wasn't the idea of Gem with another man that made him so angry.

It was the idea of not getting to watch. Or take part.

God, what was wrong with him that he was so desperate to see his wife with another man?

But he couldn't help it. Just the idea of four hands on her skin, of two mouths on her breasts, of bringing her to the heights of ecstasy and keeping her there, so she didn't know where the next touch was coming from, or who was inside her when, so she was mindless from the sensations. The thought of watching another man fuck her hard while he watched her face … Dan could feel his own cock straining against his jeans at the very idea.

The fantasy. Not the idea. Because fantasy was all it could ever be. He could never tell Gem what he dreamt of, what he craved. She couldn't understand.

Dan slumped against the tree, feeling the rise and tension in his body dissipate at the realisation.

Ever since they first fell in love, Gem had talked about soul mates, about how finding him was like coming home. They were meant to be together, partners, the two of them against the world. She'd despise him if she knew he wanted to bring another person into their sacred, special bond. Of course she would. Hell, he despised himself.

The calming sensation of the forest was beginning to wear off. Dan shook his head, pushed off the tree and set off down the path once more. He still had to find his wife, after all. Even if he could never tell her the truth.

It wasn't as if things were bad, though. Having Gem as his own was … God, it was precious. The most precious thing in the world, knowing she belonged with him. And he wouldn't jeopardise that for anything, of course he wouldn't.

Up ahead, Dan could hear sounds, voices. He frowned as they became clearer. Not just voices. Moans. And not just sounds. Familiar sounds, wrenched from a throat in the throes of pleasure.

His wife's throat.

For one, brief moment, Dan stopped, stock still, as his eyes widened and every drop of blood in his body flooded to his cock. He should be angry, horrified, distraught. He knew that, somewhere in the back of his brain. But here, now, all he could think was, *I have to see.*

Staggering slightly, Dan moved to the tree line, looking in at the clearing beyond. There, just metres away, the familiar form of his naked wife glowed in the sunlight. Gemma. His Gem. Her back against the trunk of a huge, old tree. Her head thrown back, eyes screwed tightly shut. Her legs wrapped around the waist of a stranger, a man with a strange leaf tattoo running down his back.

He couldn't help himself. Dan's hand flew to the buttons of his jeans, ripping them apart in his desperation to have his cock in his hand. Already so damn close, Dan stroked himself in time to the coupling before him, feeling his orgasm rise in him as he heard Gem spiralling closer. *Any moment now, any moment ...*

The hitch in her breath, in her moans, that always told him when she was about to come. The cry he always heard as she tensed around him. And the unfamiliar roar of the man in the glade, as he came, deep inside Dan's wife ... The combination sent Dan over the edge, faster, harder, more all encompassing than he'd imagined possible. Slumping back down in the shadows, Dan allowed himself one more moment of amazement, and recovery, before he cleaned himself up as best as he could, tucked himself back into his jeans, and forced his wobbly legs to carry him back towards the bridge.

He had a lot to think about, before Gem got home.

It was only as she crossed the bridge back to the Green Man that the magnitude of what she'd done hit Gemma.

I cheated on my husband. I had sex with another man.

Gem grabbed the wooden rail of the bridge with trembling fingers. All the arguments she'd marshalled in the woods fell away, and horror started to rise up within her. So what if Jack wasn't quite of this world? He'd felt real enough moving inside her.

And that wasn't even the worst part.

The worst part was that, as fantastic as it had felt, Jack thrusting into her, pounding her back against the tree, the thing that had tipped her over the edge, sending her into an orgasm so strong her vision went blurry ... was imagining that Dan was out there in the woods, watching her.

What is wrong with me?

'I love my husband,' Gem said, the affirmation coming out clear in the humid, still air.

'I'm very glad to hear it.'

Gem's head jerked up at the sound of Dan's voice, and she saw him, standing in the sunlight outside the pub, empty pint glasses in hand. He tipped his head to one side as he watched her.

'You OK?' he asked, and the love in his voice sent shame flooding through Gem's body.

She gave him a tight smile. 'Much better, thanks. Sorry I was gone so long.'

'No worries.' Dan shrugged. 'It picked up a bit this afternoon, but overall … it's still been pretty quiet here today. In fact …' he put the glasses down on a tray sat on the picnic table. 'I reckon we might even get an early night, if we're lucky.'

Gem's smile faltered, even as she said, 'That'd be lovely.' Fortunately, Dan had already turned to pick up another couple of glasses and didn't notice that her expression didn't match her words. How could she go to bed with her husband tonight, let him touch her, inside her, without telling him what she'd done?

He'd hate her, she knew it. That jealous streak of his … he'd never understand the need she'd felt, the desperation to have Jack, to have both of them.

She scrubbed a hand across her forehead. She had no idea how she'd got into this mess, and even less idea how she was going to get out of it again.

In stark contrast to her guilty, preoccupied mood, Dan appeared on top of the world that evening. A group of lads came in as the evening started to cool, along with a couple more locals, and Dan served them all with joyous smiles and loud greetings. Gem watched him go about his work, his grins quick and bright, his muscles shifting under his T-shirt, and wondered how she could ever have thought of being with another man, whether Jack was purely fantasy or not.

Then she remembered the feel of Jack's hands, Jack's body, holding her up against the tree as he pounded into her, and her eyes closed in confusion.

'You all right over there?' Dan asked, his voice floating across the bar to her, and Gem's eyes fluttered open again.

'I'm fine,' she said, managing a small smile. 'Just tired.'

Dan frowned, pacing over to her in a few long strides. 'You sure? If you want to head up to bed, I can manage this lot on my own. Not long until close, anyhow.'

Gem shook her head. 'Nah, I'll make it. Don't worry.'

Leaning closer, Dan raised an eyebrow. 'Don't want to go to bed without me, huh?'

'Never,' Gem said. And it was the truth. If she let her imagination run wild without Dan there, who knew what strange new fantasies she might come up with.

But Dan took it as a sign of another sort of need.

Whispering close to her ear, he said, 'I bet you're wet for me right now.'

Gem shivered, as Dan's hand curled around the back of her thigh. They were behind the bar, hidden to well above the waist. No one could see. But still, having him touch her so intimately, so close to so many other people ... if she hadn't been wet before, she certainly was now.

His fingers walked up the back of her leg, under her skirt, and Gem swallowed. How did they look, if one of the customers looked over? Like they were talking? Hugging? Whispering secrets?

Could they tell that her husband's thumb had just brushed against the edge of her knickers?

'Dan, we should ...' she started, but trailed off at the wicked look in his dark eyes.

'Shhh,' he whispered back, as his finger dipped into her underwear, sweeping along the length of her. 'God, you are wet, aren't you.'

Biting her lip, Gem nodded.

'Bet you'd like me to make you come, right here, with all these people near, wouldn't you?'

She would, Gem realised. She really would. It didn't matter that none of the customers were paying them any attention at all. The crowd of lads were playing darts in the corner, two of the locals were engrossed in a game of dominos, and the other seemed to be asleep. Nobody cared what they were doing.

But if this was the closest Gem could get to her fantasy, having Dan while someone else watched, even if they didn't join in … then she'd take it.

'Yes,' she said, her voice faint, and Dan's eyes and smile widened at the same time.

'Better be quiet, then.'

She was backed into the corner of the bar, half in the shadows, but Gem tried to school her face all the same, as Dan's fingers flicked across her clit, then curled into her. It wouldn't take much, Gem knew. She'd been on the edge all day, all week, ever since they arrived. It was all she could think about. It didn't matter that Jack had been inside her just hours before, making her come so damn hard. She still needed her husband.

Dan pressed his long, clever fingers deeper into her, curving forward to hit that spot that always made her scream. He smirked as her teeth sank into her lip, her body pulsing and contracting around him. God, it felt so damn good – and it still wasn't anywhere near enough. She leant her head against his shoulder for a moment as she recovered. She was going to go insane with wanting. That was all there was to it.

'Think that'll keep you going until bedtime?' Dan asked, his voice low. The slight tremor in it told her that he wasn't entirely unaffected by what they'd just done, either.

'If you can last that long,' she said, smiling up at him.

Dan glanced out across the mostly empty pub. 'Maybe

we can close up early tonight.'

It didn't take too long to clear out the pub, not when Dan had that kind of motivation to get him moving. Just the thought of Gem biting down on her lip as she came, hidden only by the wood of the bar ... God, it made him hard just remembering.

It was definitely way, way past their bedtime.

She had been unsure, he realised, slowing his movements as he locked up the front door. Because of what she'd done in the woods, he supposed. And so she should be. Under normal circumstances, he'd be furious, heartbroken. She should be feeling guilty.

Except ... he didn't want her to. He wanted her to want to do it again. Just with him, too, next time.

He shook his head. One step at a time. There was no way to set Gem's mind at rest without letting on that he'd been watching. So for now, he'd have to settle for reminding her how fantastic they were together, how much he loved her. Until he could find a way to broach the subject that wouldn't send her running for the hills. Or the woods.

So. First things first. Maybe he'd let her work out some of that guilt. And then maybe he'd show her he didn't care, that he loved her anyway.

After all, actions spoke louder than words, right?

Upstairs, he found Gem already in bed, and he could see she was naked beneath the thin white sheet. She was waiting for him, he realised. He smiled, and set to stripping off his own clothes as quickly as he could.

He barely made it to the edge of the bed before Gem's delicate hand shot out, running up his thigh, pulling him closer. His legs hit the mattress at the same moment her hand reached his hard cock, licking her lips as she bent her head to kiss it, then swirl her tongue around the head, wet and filthy and hungry. Just the way he liked it.

But not tonight. 'God, love, that's good,' he said, putting

124

one hand on her shoulder, guiding her back onto the mattress. 'But I need to be inside you.'

The smile she gave him was wanton. 'How do you want me?' she asked, quirking her lips, but Dan could see the guilt hovering behind her eyes. She was trying to make it up to him, and he couldn't even tell her there was nothing to be guilty about.

'Get on your knees,' he said, voice hoarse. She looked a little surprised, but obeyed without question for once, which he was grateful for. It wasn't an entirely selfish request: he knew she loved the way his cock pressed forward inside her when she was on all fours. But more importantly, he wouldn't have to look at the guilt in his wife's eyes as he fucked her.

We can't go on like this, he realised, as Gem glanced back over her shoulder at him. He needed to find a way to talk to her, to admit what he'd seen, and confess all the things he wanted, needed.

But not tonight. Tonight he just wanted to lose himself in her, to feel her all around him, to come so hard inside her, like the man in the woods had done.

Just the memory was enough to send him lurching forward, grabbing Gem's hips rougher than he'd intended to, pulling her back onto his cock where he stood, at the side of the bed. He sank into her in one, swift movement, and his eyes squeezed shut at the feeling of her, so hot and wet and tight around him.

Gem moaned as he pulled back again, but it sounded muffled, for some reason. He opened his eyes, then blinked hard at the sight before him. There, kneeling on the other side of the mattress, was the man from the woods, unearthly in his perfection, tattoo stretching over his shoulder, his hard cock in Gem's mouth.

Dan's grip on her hips tightened as he fought to keep from coming there and then. God, was he so desperate to share her that he was hallucinating, now?

The other man reached forward, under Gem's body, to twist her nipples, and Dan decided he didn't care. Hallucination, dream, wishful thinking … whatever it was, it was too good to waste.

Yanking Gem's body back as he thrust forward, Dan sank deep into her again, watching as her lips moved down the length of the man's cock. He had his head thrown back now, and Dan could see his Adam's apple bob as he swallowed. Dan hitched his hips forward once more, and Gem swallowed the other cock down as he pushed her on to it.

God … this … this … this ... This was what he'd wanted, all this time. All he wanted.

He couldn't hold back any more, not with such an erotic sight laid out before him, real or not. Letting go, he pumped in and out of Gem's body, faster and faster, his grip on her hips hauling her onto his cock time and again, his gaze locked on her mouth as it moved over that other cock, taking it so deep he was half afraid she might choke, then releasing it so that only the tip sat between her lips.

He had to have this for real. He had to see her do this outside his imagination.

Tomorrow, he promised himself. Tomorrow, he'd take her to the woods, and tell her what he knew. What he'd seen, and what he wanted.

Tomorrow, his dream might come true.

With that thought, he let his hand drift down over Gem's hip, brushing against her clit, just lightly. It was enough, though. With another muffled moan, she fell apart under him, her pussy clenching and clamping down on his cock. Dan groaned as her orgasm tipped him over the edge, and he came, hard and long, deep inside her.

And as he looked up, he caught the eye of the other man, saw his mouth open in a silent cry, as he emptied himself into Gem's mouth.

Tomorrow, Dan thought again as he collapsed against

Gem's back on the bed, the apparition floating away.
   Tomorrow, he'd make this happen for real.

Chapter Seven

THE NEXT DAY WAS Saturday, and the pub was filled with walkers and weekenders staying nearby. Gem served drinks and snacks and tried not to think about the way Jack had intruded on another night with Dan. Would she never be able to have sex with her husband again, without imagining her fantasy man there with them? But with Dan fucking her from behind … all she'd been able to think about was having Jack in her mouth at the same time.

Dan had been quiet most of the day, but they'd been too busy for her to figure out why. But as the evening drew on, the crowds thinned, until there were only a couple of locals left, and Gem knew they'd both be gone before ten.

'If you wanted, we could probably close up early again tonight,' Dan said, surveying the pub from beside her. 'Maybe take a walk in the woods together.'

Gem's heart pounded at the thought. What if Jack was there? What if … Oh God, *what if …?*

'That might be nice,' she managed. Maybe it wasn't such a bad idea. After all, things always seemed to make sense in the woods. It was only once she left that reality came crashing down.

Dan nodded. 'OK, then. Let's start getting cleared up here. Soon as these two head home, we'll go.'

No other customers had come in by the time the pub was cleared, and, as the sun finally started its descent behind the trees, their last customers left, and Gem followed Dan out of the pub, apprehension twisting in her gut. She paused before the doorway, taking a moment to stare at the carved face of the Green Man on the wall. It was Jack, so obvious now when she looked, and Gem couldn't believe she hadn't seen it from the start.

He looked like he was laughing at her. That should have been a giveaway.

'Come on,' Dan called from the bridge, and Gem hurried to catch up.

In the fading daylight, the woods were even cooler. Dan threw an arm around her shoulder and Gem snuggled closer; it was a relief just to be close without overheating. Maybe a walk in the woods was a good idea. Maybe it would be fine, just the two of them. Romantic, even. Jack wouldn't approach if she was with Dan, would he?

Except, of course, she'd told him that was exactly what she wanted – the two of them together.

Gem shivered at the thought, and Dan's arm tightened around her.

'You can't possibly be cold,' he said, leaning in so his words brushed against her cheek.

'Not cold,' Gem confirmed. 'Just … I don't know.'

Dan's hand slipped from her shoulder, running down her body to her waist, her hip, squeezing and holding her close against his side. 'Bet I do.'

Gem opened her mouth to ask exactly what he meant by that, but before she could speak, she realised where they were. She hadn't been paying enough attention, so distracted by the thought of Jack waiting for them in the woods. Stupid mistake. She should have led Dan the other way, followed a different path. But she hadn't, and now …

Now they were standing on the edge of her clearing.

And Jack was watching them from the side of the stream.

'Gemma,' Jack said, his voice like the wind in the trees, and so full of wanting Dan had to be able to hear it.

Dan's hand pushed against her bottom, propelling her into the glade so she stood between the two men. Thoughts tumbled through her brain faster than she could turn them

129

into words. She needed to explain, to salvage the situation, she needed to say something before Jack did, she needed to …

'It's all right, Gem.' Dan's soft words from behind her calmed the tumult in her head, just a little.

'I can explain,' she said.

'You don't need to.' Turning, she saw Dan was staring at Jack as he spoke. 'I saw you, yesterday afternoon.'

Oh God. Oh God, oh God, oh God. 'Dan, it wasn't … I mean, it was –'

'It was the hottest thing I'd ever seen,' Dan said, and Gemma's whole world stopped.

Glancing over at Jack, Gem saw his knowing smile and laughing eyes and thought, *Yeah, no help there.* Turning back to Dan, all she could see was the want, the need in his eyes.

'I was imagining you were watching,' she said, and Dan lunged forward, taking her face between his hands as he kissed her, hard and deep.

'God, I loved watching you so much,' he murmured, between kisses. 'I'd always wanted … but I never dreamt I'd get to see it.'

'I thought you'd hate me,' Gem said, relief making her legs weak. 'I just … it wasn't until I got home I even realised what I'd done.'

'It's these woods,' Dan said, trailing his lips down her neck and making her shiver again. 'It's like they make you admit all your most hidden fantasies.'

Gem jerked away, her head snapping back to look at Jack behind them. 'It's you, isn't it? You're doing this.'

Jack spread his hands in front of him, a show of innocence, as he took a step closer towards them. 'What little power I have, is confined to these woods. And even here, all I can make you do is acknowledge the truth of your desires.'

'The old man tried to tell me …' Gem trailed off,

remembering.

'The families that have lived in this area for centuries, they remember what these woods are for. And they visit, sometimes.'

'And do you entertain yourself with them as well?' Dan asked, and Gem felt his arms wrap around her waist, making her feel safe.

The smugness faded from Jack's face and suddenly, he was an entirely different man. No longer the confident seducer Gem remembered from the day before. Not even the fantasy man from her imaginings in the pub. Now, Jack looked every bit as unsure of things as she felt.

'No …' he said, the word soft. 'Not like this. Not ever … Usually, it's just my influence they need, just the opportunity to make things happen for themselves. They need the feel of the woods, the weight of the history here, the fertility rites, the lovers who have come before them. But you …' his eyes met Gem's and what she saw there took her breath away. 'You were different. You wanted me, from that first night …'

'When I saw you on the bridge.' She looked up at Dan. 'He was watching us, that first night in the pub. That's what started this.'

Dan frowned. 'But you hadn't been in the woods then.' He looked up at Jack. 'I thought you said –'

'I did nothing but watch,' Jack interrupted. 'I … felt your presence, nearby. It compelled me to travel to the edge of my forest and see for myself.' His eyes caught Gem's and held them, and she sucked in a deep breath. 'Everything you imagined that night, and every night since, you came to of your own volition.'

She heard Dan's breathing hitch behind her. 'You really want this?' he asked. 'You really want both of us?'

Gem twisted in his arms so he could see the truth on her face. 'So much. Do you?'

'God yes. Yesterday … I loved watching. But I wanted to

131

join you both, more than anything.'

Hands settled on her waist, and Gem glanced up over her shoulder to see Jack behind her, leaving enough space between them that she could step away if she wanted. But she didn't want, not at all. So instead, she wriggled backwards and felt his hard cock pressing against her backside. Her hands on Dan's hips, she pulled him closer too, so she could feel his erection against her stomach. Perfect.

'Both of you,' she said. 'I need both of you.'

Apparently that was all the encouragement her men needed. Heat flooded her body as they worked together to strip off her shirt, her skirt, her underwear, until she stood naked in the middle of the glade. The need in her body was overwhelming. Every inch of her skin craved their touch, every muscle in her body wanted to move against them. This was every fantasy she'd ever had come true, and she intended to savour every last moment of it.

Jack's hands started at her shoulders, working their way down over her back to her hips, even as Dan's fingers moved up her stomach towards her breasts. Lifting her lips, she kissed Dan firmly, then twisted her head to kiss Jack as well, as Dan leant to take one nipple in his mouth. Gem moaned against Jack's lips at the sensations coursing through her body.

With a chuckle, Jack swept a hand across her hip, down to her thigh, bringing his fingers right up to her centre. Without warning he plunged one finger into her, sliding easily into her wetness, as his thumb came up to circle her clit. Gasping, Gem rested her head against Dan's shoulder as he straightened, releasing her breast, only to send his own hand down to join Jack's.

'Oh God,' she moaned against Dan's shirt, as Jack's thumb pulled away to let Dan's fingers take over. 'More. Please.'

'Your every wish,' Jack said, as he added an extra finger

inside her, curling them against her with beautiful pressure. 'That's what we're here for.'

'Then I wish,' Gem gasped, as Dan's fingers picked up speed on her clit and tremors started to build inside her. 'I wish that the two of you were as naked as I am.'

'Just one … more … moment …' Dan said, and Gem broke, her body clenching and releasing as she cried out.

Her legs felt like cotton, soft and unsteady. Jack and Dan laid her down on the grass, matching smirks on their faces as she looked up at them.

'Shouldn't you two be stripping already,' Gem asked, stretching against the springy moss and grass of the river bank. 'We're not nearly done here.'

Jack and Dan shed clothes in record time, but then held back, still watching her. Gem realised her hand had come up to knead her breast as she stared at the reveal of their bodies.

'How do you …?' Dan trailed off, eyes still burning as he gazed at her.

'What would you have us do?' Jack asked, dropping to his knees beside her and reaching out to massage her other breast. 'How can we best please you?'

The sight of Jack's hands on her body clearly galvanised Dan into action. Before Gem even realised he'd moved, she felt his hands pushing her knees apart, and his tongue stroking her folds open, tasting her.

'God, I'm so …' Gem started, but the words faded in her throat.

'You're so sensitive right now,' Jack said for her, his voice low and husky. 'I can … sense the emotions, the sensations loose in the forest. I can feel how your body trembles inside. How your skin tingles and sparks. I can feel … everything.'

Gem looked up at her dream lover and knew it was true. His eyes were half closed with lust, his cock jutting out hard and thick between them. And as Dan licked deep into her, his strong tongue flicking up over her clit, her body jerked off the ground at the contact, and she realised that Jack's had done the same.

He was experiencing everything she was. Gem smiled. What if he were to experience even more?

Without giving him any warning, she turned her head and ran her tongue up the line of Jack's cock, before taking the head into her mouth. Down between her thighs, Dan stopped moving for a moment, then replaced his tongue with his finger, lazily circling her clit, and Gem knew he was watching them.

Lust surged through her body. More than the feel of their hands on her, more than the weight of Jack's cock against her tongue, the thought of Dan watching made her nipples harder and her belly tighten. She'd wanted two men. And now she had them, she was going to enjoy every second.

Reaching over with one hand to grip the base of Jack's cock, Gem shifted up on to her knees, taking care never to stop moving her mouth over him. Behind her, Dan moved against her, hands on her hips, pulling her up into a kneeling position. Jack groaned at the feel of her hand and mouth, and Gem felt so powerful she couldn't help but smile around him.

Dan's hardness rubbed against her wet folds and her smile turned into a moan. This was it. This was how it should have been last night, if Jack had really been there. Her pussy clenched in anticipation, desperate to feel her husband inside her again. She gasped, squeezing Jack tighter as the head of Dan's cock began to push into her, inch by tantalising inch, stretching her the way she loved best.

Jack's hands settled on her head, clenching in her hair, and Gem realised he was feeling this, too. God, it must be so overwhelming for him. He'd said he'd never taken part before, just absorbed the feelings in the forest. How new, how incredible, this must feel for him.

She moaned again as Dan finally, finally, thrust fully inside her. It was pretty damn incredible for her; she had no idea how Jack was holding off coming. *Guess being an ancient forest being teaches you patience.*

But that was the last complete thought she could manage, as Dan pulled out, so far that only the very tip of him was still inside her. Gem felt bereft, empty for a long moment, until Dan slammed home again, pushing her forward so she had no choice but to swallow Jack deeper down. It was enough to send Jack careering over the edge, at last. He cried out, a deep, guttural sound, his hands clutching Gem closely to him. Gem suckled at him a moment longer, swallowing down every last salty drop, before his hands loosened, and he sat back, looking down at her with awe.

'That was …' he started, but Dan interrupted, saying, 'Not over yet.'

Still deep inside her, he pulled Gem back against him, away from Jack. Gem put out her hands to brace herself on the ground, not sure what her husband was planning. Glancing over her shoulder, she saw him settle, lying down on the ground, his hands on her hips keeping him sheathed within her.

'Put your knees either side of me,' Dan said, grinning up at her. Gem obeyed, feeling his cock moving inside her, pressing forward in a way that made her clit burn. 'Now … move.'

Her knees still a little wobbly, Gem raised herself up then plunged back down on top of Dan, hearing him groan behind her. Looking up, she caught Jack's eyes, then let her gaze trail down his beautiful body, to where his cock was hardening again. Behind her, Dan's hands settled on her hips, helping her set the pace as she rose and fell, each drop filling her so perfectly she wanted to scream.

Without conscious thought, Gem's hands reached up to cup her breasts, holding them as if for Jack's inspection. He lurched forward a little at the sight, and Gem smiled, twisting her nipples between her fingertips, the sensation sending jolts down her body, straight to her clit. Her eyes fluttered closed for a moment, flying open again when she felt Jack's lips nudging her left hand away, as he wrapped his mouth around her breast, sucking in as much of it as would fit.

Dan's hands were the only thing keeping the rhythm going now, pulling her down onto him hard as he thrust up to meet her. Gem's head lolled back as she let the sensations run over her, through her, wondering what Jack made of the way her body vibrated at the feel of the two of them, loving her.

Jack's mouth switched to her other breast, his tongue running circles round her sensitive nipple. Gem groaned as he sucked it into her mouth, then pulled off with a pop. He chuckled at her unspoken objection, running kisses down the soft flesh of her belly, down lower, and lower. It took real effort for Gem to open her eyes and watch him go, but it was worth it to see him kneeling between Dan's legs, hands braced on her husband's thighs as he lowered his mouth to where they were joined.

Gem fought against Dan's hands, keeping him deep inside her as Jack's tongue swirled around her clit. But the sparks that flooded her body made her pliable, and Dan lifted her up again to continue their rhythm. This time, though, when she slammed back down again, Jack was waiting for her, licking against her and making her muscles tighten and tighten. She wasn't going to be able to take this very long. Especially if ... Dan groaned, and she looked down to see Jack's tongue pressing up the length of her husband's cock before he reached her.

Too much. It was too much, too hot, too fantastic. Gem's hands clutched her knees as she bore down, grinding hard against Dan as she felt him spasm under her, coming deep inside her even as Jack's tongue took her over the edge. Her body contracted and clenched, holding Dan tight inside her as she came around him, her whole self shaking.

Jack caught her in his arms as she tumbled forward,

holding her close against his chest. Dan slid out of her, looking dazed as he sat up. Gem gave him a tired smile, then pushed Jack forward on to the ground, curling up against his side. Dan was tucked in behind her in moments, his warm body crushing her against Jack's cooler one, his breaths deepening in sleep almost instantly. Gem blinked up at her dream lover, wondering how she could be so lucky as to have him be real. Running her hand down his chest, enjoying the hard planes of his body, her fingers brushed against his still hard cock.

'I'm sorry,' she said, her words blurring with tiredness. 'I should …'

Jack kissed the top of her head. 'You should sleep. We've got all night ahead of us.'

Gem looked up at the sky, darkening in between the branches of the trees, and fell asleep imagining how many ways she could enjoy her men before sunrise.

Chapter Eight

LATER, MUCH LATER, WHEN Gem's bones felt like liquid, and her blood hummed with satisfaction, she twisted onto her side atop the dewy grass, grateful for the cool even in the heat of the night, and found Dan watching her.

'You OK?' The words were whispered, barely a sound on the breeze, but even in the darkness she lay close enough to see the concern in his eyes.

'More than,' she assured him. Glancing back over her shoulder, she saw Jack's bare chest rising and falling in a slow, even rhythm. They'd worn him out, at last. She snuggled closer to Dan, feeling his arm wrap around her, holding her loosely against him.

'Me too,' he said, answering her unasked question. 'I didn't think ... I couldn't have imagined that I could have this.'

Gem chuckled against his skin. 'I didn't even imagine I could want it. Until we came to the Green Man.'

The muscles of his chest tightened under her cheek. 'What?' she asked, then listened to him breathe through a long pause. But she knew her husband, knew how his mind worked. He wasn't not answering, he was figuring out how to say it.

'I think I always knew,' he said, eventually. 'I didn't want to admit it to myself. But I've always wanted to see you with another man.'

'But you didn't tell me.' Gem tried to keep her tone neutral, not accusing. It didn't matter now, not really, and it wasn't as if she didn't have her own secrets.

'I couldn't.' Dan's arm tightened around her, and he kissed the top of her head. 'You were too precious, too important. I needed you more than I wanted anything else. As long as I had you … the rest of it didn't matter. Until we came here.'

'Jack's influence,' Gem said with a smile. 'He sure is potent.'

'But you're right,' Dan went on as if she hadn't spoken. 'If we're going to do this … we can't have secrets between us, any more. There's too much at risk. If either of us … well …'

'Changes our mind?' Gem shook her head, her hair brushing against his skin. 'I don't think that's very likely, do you?' Not after the incredible night they'd had. Not when everything felt so damn right, for the first time in so long.

'No, I don't. But still …'

'Yeah, I know. No secrets.' Gem sucked in a deep breath, and found courage in the dim light of the almost dawn. 'In which case, I have to tell you something. I know why we were banished to the Green Man.'

'You do?' The surprise in Dan's voice made her look up. 'You know about Mark's offer?'

Gem frowned. 'Offer? More of a demand, I thought. And yeah, of course I know about it. I was the one in the cellar refusing him.'

Dan's arms went rigid, and his voice when he spoke again sounded dark, dangerous. 'What did he do to you?'

'He tried to persuade me to sleep with him, and when I said no he tried to unbutton my blouse.' Gem shrugged, trying to play it as nonchalant as she could. She needed Dan to know it didn't matter any more. Nothing did, except being there, with him and with Jack. 'I kneed him in the balls and whacked him over the head with a cocktail shaker, if that helps.'

The tension in Dan's body started to ebb away, and Gem bent her lips to touch against the warm skin of his chest. 'It does help. I thought it was my fault.'

'Your fault?' Gem murmured the question against his body, engrossed once more with the way he tasted, the way he felt against her mouth. 'Why?'

'Because Mark Fisher offered me any pub I wanted, if I let him have one night with you. Even said I could watch.'

Gem blinked. That, she hadn't expected. Although, it made perfect sense, when you considered that Mark Fisher was a slimy snake. 'You turned him down?'

'Of course I bloody did!'

'I mean … even though you knew you wanted to see me with another man?'

'Not him.' The vehemence in Dan's voice made Gem's heart beat a little faster. 'Never him.'

'Good.' Returning to kissing her way across her husband's body, Gem couldn't help but ask, 'Was it everything you hoped for? With Jack?'

Dan's arm, wrapped around her waist, hauled her up so she lay across him. 'And so much more. God, Gem, it was …'

'I know.' Sitting up, straddling him, Gem felt the firm pressure of Dan's cock pressing into her. He was hard again, just thinking about it, she realised. Moisture flooded her pussy as she brushed along the length of him, sinking down onto him in one perfectly natural movement.

Dan groaned as she started to move, slowly, languorously. 'God, you feel good.'

Gem chuckled. 'Want me to wake Jack up?'

'Let him sleep.' Dan ran his hands up her thighs, pressing both thumbs against her clit as he reached the top. 'He probably needs his rest after all we've put him through tonight.'

'Not to mention what I've got planned for tomorrow.' Gem's belly tightened as Dan began to stroke against her, and she began to move a little faster, chasing that spiral up to perfect pleasure.

'Can't wait,' Dan said, and smiled up at her, pure happiness, completeness in his eyes.

Gem bit her lip as she realised. Nothing felt like it was missing now. She didn't need a dream lover, because she knew they had Jack, when he woke up. There were no secrets any more, nothing between them, no unspoken desires. She looked over and saw Jack, awake now and watching them, stroking his own hard cock, waiting his turn.

It felt perfect, she realised, as Dan pressed harder into her, and her body broke apart around him.

Absolutely perfect.

In the end, the sun was already most of the way to its highest point by the time the three of them made their unsteady way out of the woods. Gem's body ached from the soles of her feet to the smile that stretched across her face, and she simply could not care. Her muscles felt so relaxed she was amazed she was still standing. In fact, if it hadn't been for Dan's arm around her shoulders, and Jack's grip on her waist, she might not be.

'Do we have to open the pub today?' she asked, leaning her head against her husband's shoulder. 'Can't we all just go back to bed?'

Dan laughed, the chuckle vibrating through his chest. 'For how long, exactly? Don't you think the brewery might get a little suspicious if we never open again?'

'I suppose,' Gem said. The very thought of Mark Bloody Fisher was enough to cast a cloud over her day. She looked up at her men, standing at the edge of the woods in the morning sunshine. Only a very small cloud, though.

Gem looked over at Jack, and in an instant forgot all about Mark, and the brewery, as soon as she saw the frown on Jack's face. He was staring just ahead of them, at the bridge back to the pub.

'What is it?' she asked, moving to take his hand in her own. 'Aren't you coming?' Fear rose in her chest at the very

141

idea. Had she been given everything she ever dreamt of, just to have it ripped away? Had Jack decided he didn't want this after all? Could she go back to just the two of them, for the rest of her life?

Jack's smile was sad. 'I only wish I could. When I told you, my powers extend only to the edges of the forest ...'

Dan put it together first, and his amusement vanished. 'You can't leave.'

'This bridge is the furthest I can travel.' Jack took a step backwards, away from them, and Gem reached out and grabbed his hand instinctively. She couldn't let him fade back into the forest. What if she never saw him again?

She looked up at Dan, not entirely sure what he read in her eyes as he studied her. But then he nodded, and Gem knew that was all she needed.

'Then we'll come back to you,' she promised. 'Tonight, after we close. You won't be always alone any more, Jack.'

Jack's eyes slid away from hers, up to Dan's, and whatever he saw there convinced him. 'Tonight, then.'

'And every night,' Gem pressed.

Jack glanced between them again, then nodded, a small smile on his lips. 'As often as you want me, I will be there. You know where to find me, after all.'

He bent to kiss Gem, his lips soft against hers, and despite the lengthy night and the ache that permeated her every cell, Gem still felt a familiar heat starting to rise in her, before he pulled away. He turned next to Dan, raising one eyebrow at him.

Dan smirked. 'See you tonight,' was all he said. Gem let out a disappointed breath. She supposed it might take a little time, but she had hope ... one day she'd get to see her men kiss, and touch, just as they both kissed and touched her.

She had plenty of time, after all. They weren't going anywhere.

The phone was ringing behind the bar as they stepped

through the door. Gem gave Dan a tired smile as she moved forward to answer it. Back to the real world, apparently. 'Green Man pub?'

'Gemma, my darling.' Mark Fisher's oily tones were all the more odious for interrupting her perfect morning after, Gem decided.

'Mark,' she said, scowling at Dan.

'I've decided to offer you a compromise,' Mark said. 'Since you're not ready to see things entirely my way, just yet.'

'A compromise?' On the other side of the bar, Dan raised his eyebrows as she repeated the words.

'Exactly. You and your darling Daniel can come and work at my new pub in London. Conveniently situated just around the corner from my office.' Mark's smirk was almost audible. 'I'm sure I can convince you to see things my way, in time.'

Gem thought about Jack, waiting for them in the woods. Thought of the way Dan had smiled at her when he woke for the first time that morning. Thought about all the nights she had to come ahead of her.

'No thanks, Mark. We're far happier here at the Green Man.'

Then she hung up the phone and kissed her husband across the bar.

Off the Shelf
by Lucy Felthouse

Chapter One

PUSHING THE "ON" BUTTON, Annalise moved the vibrator down between her parted legs and eased it inside her eager pussy. As the ears of the *Rampant Rabbit* slid into position on her clit, she groaned with pleasure and rolled her hips, desperate to get more delicious friction. Then she pressed another button on the toy's control panel to ramp up the power another notch. As much as she'd prefer a slower build-up to her orgasm, she just didn't have the time. She had to leave for the airport in a couple of hours, and she hadn't even packed her case. A quick knee-trembler would have to suffice.

As the vibrator buzzed away between her thighs, Annalise closed her eyes and tried to empty her mind of everything but the pleasure she was experiencing. After a brief flirtation with the thought that she'd much prefer a hot man between her legs bringing her to orgasm, Annalise simply enjoyed the feeling of her impending climax. The busily-vibrating bunny ears pressed tightly against her sensitive flesh soon had her pussy fluttering. Then, without warning, Annalise was quickly yanked onto her pleasure plateau and immediately pushed off, leaving her writhing and shouting on the bed as a powerful orgasm overtook her body.

She arched her back as waves of pleasure crashed over

her, and her pussy clenched and grabbed at the toy buried deep inside. Her swollen clit throbbed, quickly becoming too sensitive for the unrelenting stimulation from the vibrator. Switching it off and pulling out, Annalise dropped the toy onto the mattress by her side and gave a satisfied moan as she rode out the remainder of her climax. Finally, when the twitches and spasms had abated and her heart rate and breathing were almost back to normal, Annalise grabbed the *Rabbit* and rolled across to the side of her bed where the toy box was kept. She made short but thorough work of cleaning it, then reluctantly put it in its case, popped it into the small bedside cupboard and shut the door.

Annalise hated leaving her favourite toy behind when she went away, but she just wasn't brave enough to take it with her. She usually only took carry-on luggage, and the very thought of the distinctive shape of the *Rampant Rabbit* popping up on the screen of the airport scanners made her shudder. It would be bad enough for the staff to see it on their monitors, knowing what it was and giving her knowing looks; imagine what would happen if they decided to check inside her bags! She would want to curl up and die of embarrassment, she just knew it.

No, it was much better off staying here. She could make do with her right hand for a few days. Even better, she might meet someone. Annalise smiled. She'd had some pretty steamy encounters on her travels: the desk clerk in Dubai; the gym manager in Turkey; the waiter in Corfu ...

Annalise shook herself. This wasn't the time to let her mind wander down that path and get herself all worked up. She had to go and get ready now. There'd be plenty of time for daydreaming later, when she was in long and boring queues, and on the flight.

Just as she was about to head into the bathroom, Annalise's phone rang. Retrieving the handset from its cradle on her bedside cabinet, she glanced at the caller display before putting the phone to her ear.

'Hi, Mum,' she said, trying to keep the exasperation out of her voice. Her mother often called when she was short of time, and it was always a struggle to get her off the line without upsetting her. 'You all right?'

'Yes, dear. Everything's fine. I'm just calling to wish you a safe journey. Where is it you're going this time?'

'Portugal, Mum. Just for a few days.'

'Portugal. Lovely. I expect you'll get a nice tan.'

Annalise rolled her eyes. She'd given up trying to explain to her parents that she wasn't going off on free holidays all the time. It was *work*. Granted, it was very nice work, getting to travel all over the world and write about hotels, holiday destinations and tourist attractions for a living, but nonetheless it was work. She didn't have time for lying around on beaches and sunbathing. She could see the article now:

Such and such hotel complex is sublime. Spacious, clean and luxurious, it deserves each one of its five stars. The restaurants and foods are wonderful, and the spa is a total haven of relaxation. The beautiful sandy beach is a suntrap and has umbrellas and sunbeds, and its own bar.

And that would be pretty much it. Naturally, each of Annalise's projects varied, but on the whole she was expected to go somewhere and write a piece on the complete package; the location, accommodation, and surrounding area. How on earth could she pen an emotive piece about the monastery high up in the hills if she never left the beach? She was good, but not that good.

'Yes, Mum, I expect I will.'

'And you might even meet a man. Portuguese, eh?' She paused, and Annalise gritted her teeth ready for the inevitable onslaught. 'Oh yes, very loyal the Portuguese. Family orientated. Wonderful marriage material.'

It took every ounce of self control Annalise had not to

147

start banging her head on the wall. They had this chat on a regular basis. Well, actually, Annalise's mother had this chat *at* Annalise on a regular basis. She lived in eternal hope that her daughter would come home from one of her trips with a man in tow, following a whirlwind romance, and they'd declare they couldn't live without each other and were to be married as soon as possible.

'Yes, Mum.' Annalise replied, no longer bothering to keep the boredom out of her voice. 'Anyway, I'd better go. I need to pack. Call you when I'm back.'

'Now, don't take that tone with me. I'm only looking out for your interests. You're not getting any younger, are you? You don't want to be left on the shelf.'

'Bye, Mum. Love you.'

Dropping the phone back into its cradle, Annalise pulled a face at it before walking into the bathroom and turning on the shower. As she waited for the water to reach temperature, she couldn't help but think about her mother's words.

Her whole family were the same. They constantly asked when she was going to settle down, get married and have children. She was utterly fed up with the comments about "not getting any younger" and being "like *Bridget Jones*". She couldn't seem to make them understand that she *did* want to do all of those things. Of course she wanted someone to share her life – and her bed – but she needed to meet someone first. Unfortunately, just as her job didn't leave much time for sunbathing, it also didn't leave much time for meeting men. Ones suitable for something more than a one-night-stand, anyway.

At least they'd stopped setting her up. After a chain of absolute disasters and many sharp words, there'd been no more random sons, brothers, work friends and the like turning up at family get-togethers. Annalise was grateful for this small mercy. Some of them had been so horrific she was offended her family had even thought they would be suitable

148

for her. Was she really that undesirable?

It didn't assuage her annoyance at the whole situation, though. It frustrated the hell out of Annalise that she was 35 years old and had a very successful career that she'd worked hard to build up, and yet, rather than praising her for what she *did* have, her family just constantly picked up on what she didn't have. Well, stuff them, Annalise thought. I've got a bloody good job and I'm proud of what I've achieved, even if they aren't. And when I do eventually meet someone, it'll be for me, not them. I'd rather be stuck on the damn shelf forever than end up lumbered with some total tosser. Mr Right will come along at some point.

He has to.

Chapter Two

WALKING THROUGH THE SCANNER, Annalise heaved a sigh of relief as she reached the other side without a hitch. She knew the airport checks were in place for a reason, and she certainly didn't begrudge them, but it didn't stop her dreading going through. She lived in fear of being the one to set the alarm off, being pulled off to one side and checked over while everyone looked at her accusingly. She never did set the scanners off, but she was sure that one day it would be her turn.

Dashing to pick up her belongings from the conveyor belt, Annalise pulled her watch, bracelet and shoes back on, then grabbed her carry-on and made her way towards the departure lounge. She made a conscious effort not to walk too fast, thinking she'd look suspicious if she did. She knew it was utterly ridiculous, but the whole damn process made her *feel* guilty of something, even though she wasn't.

She walked past the shops selling clothes – who on earth bought clothes at the airport anyway? – toiletries and duty free, and made her way into her safe haven – the book shop.

As she stepped over the threshold, Annalise did what she did every time she entered a bookshop: she took a deep breath. The delicious smell of new books always had a calming effect on her, which was why she was glad the shop was so close to the damn airport security. Her travel schedule was always the same: arrive at airport; check in; go through security; get stressed; dash to bookshop; alleviate stress before boarding flight.

Today was no exception. Annalise moved deeper into the

store, wondering where to go first. A glance at her watch told her that she'd got through check-in in record time and had some time to kill before her flight. She smiled – extra time in the bookshop was never a bad thing. She knew it was sad, but hey, everyone has quirks, right?

Annalise made a beeline for the travel section, but just before she got there she was stopped in her tracks. Impeding her entrance to the aisle was a man. And, judging by the flutter of her heart and the heat coming to her face, a very attractive one. Annalise watched him as she waited for her rational thoughts to catch up with what her body was telling her.

Seconds later, it became apparent they were in total agreement. The man – who, judging by his attire, was a member of staff – was indeed cute. He looked to be around Annalise's age. He was taller than her, even though she wore heels, and he had a slim build. His long curly hair was tied back, and something about the way he was cradling a book in his hands made Annalise suspect she'd found a kindred spirit. He wasn't the usual tall, muscular type she went for, but she hadn't had much luck with those guys, anyway, so looking at someone a little different couldn't do any harm, could it?

She continued towards the travel section before someone saw her acting like some kind of weird bookshop voyeur. Annalise figured the guy was new here. She came into this shop often enough to know the staff, and she'd never seen him before. She'd *definitely* have remembered him.

He looked up as she drew close, a pair of intelligent green eyes behind dark-rimmed glasses adding to the guy's bookish appeal. His lips curved into a smile and he shuffled forward to let her by. Annalise gave a polite nod of thanks, moved past him and put her bag down at her feet.

Standing next to him as they both perused the shelves, Annalise caught the scent of his cologne. She had no idea what it was or how to describe it, but she did know it smelt totally divine. Almost mouth watering. Could this guy *be* any more appealing?

Reaching forward, Annalise grabbed a book from the shelf in order to distract herself before she got into trouble for sexual harassment. The two of them flicked pages in silence for a few minutes, until the quiet was suddenly broken by the sound of his voice.

'Do you know,' he said, quietly, as though they were in a library, rather than a bookshop, 'I've quite forgotten myself. I'm supposed to be working here, and here I am browsing books and completely ignoring the customers.'

He closed the book he was looking at and slid it back into place on the shelf. Turning to Annalise, he held out a hand. 'I'm Damien. I'm so sorry, I've only just started working here and I seem to keep forgetting that part. I blame the books. They distract me.'

Annalise looked down at his outstretched hand and thought how odd it was that he was introducing himself. Bookshop staff – nice as they usually were – didn't often make a habit of approaching customers and partaking in formal introductions. Not to mention the fact he was wearing a name badge, so telling her his name was completely redundant. She slipped her hand into his and shook it anyway, not wanting to appear rude.

'I'm Annalise.' She couldn't think of anything witty or interesting to say to follow that, so she dropped Damien's hand as soon as was polite and wondered whether she should grab her bag and head over to the fiction section until he'd gone. Before she could move, though, he said, 'Sorry. I'm not crazy. I just talk rubbish when I'm nervous. And I guess I was just being overly nice to stop you from going to my manager and grassing me up for reading on the job.'

Annalise struggled to suppress a smile at Damien's rambling. He was blushing, and kept touching his hands to his ears as if tucking his hair behind them, then remembering he had it tied up. She found it completely endearing, and the movement of his hands drew her attention to them, highlighting the fact that he wasn't wearing a wedding ring. It didn't mean he was unattached, of course, but at least she could plead ignorance if it did turn out he was with someone.

Finally allowing her smile, and a soft laugh, to escape, Annalise put poor Damien out of his misery.

'I'm not going to tell your manager anything. I'm a fellow book lover, I totally see the attraction.' She lowered her voice and leaned towards Damien a little, as if imparting a secret. 'And to be honest, they distract me, too. Why do you think I'm here? It's not exactly the most hip and happening place in the airport, is it?'

The two of them poked their heads out of the end of the aisle and looked around, noting the fact there was only one other customer in the shop. Aside from the bored-looking young girl on the till, that was it. Ducking back into the travel section, they laughed together, the ice thoroughly broken.

As Annalise watched Damien compose himself, she had a realisation. Despite the fact he wasn't her usual type and that he was, well ... a little odd, she really liked him. And he was hot. The dimple that appeared in his right cheek when he smiled cemented that fact. Annalise resolved to find out if they had more in common than their love of books. After all, she thought, how does the saying go? "You'll meet someone when you're least expecting it." Or was that something her mum said? *Oh, whatever.*

'So,' Damien said, his colour back to normal, though a cheeky glint remained in his eyes, 'I work here. What's your excuse for being at the airport?'

'Oh,' Annalise had been trying to think of a line of conversation, and he'd beaten her to it, 'I'm on my way to work, I guess. I'm a travel writer.'

'Really?' he replied. 'That's so interesting. Where are you off to?'

Annalise realised she still had the book she'd been flicking through in her hand and held it up so he could see the cover.

'Portugal. I've been before, but there are so many different areas and resorts ...' she tailed off. She didn't want to bore Damien with the details.

'So, if you're already booked into a no doubt very posh hotel with all the arrangements taken care of, what are you expecting to find in that book?' He didn't sound accusing, but genuinely confused.

'I don't just write about the hotels. I like to write more rounded articles, aimed at different people. Granted, all some people care about is the hotel, the weather and the food, and are content to sunbathe all day. But others want to get out into the country and experience the culture, see some tourist attractions and stuff, you know?'

'Sure,' Damien replied, nodding enthusiastically. 'I'm definitely one of the latter. I like to go and check out what's off the beaten track – the quirkier, the better.'

'Exactly!' Annalise replied, a little too loudly. She was lucky it *was* a bookshop and not a library, otherwise she'd have stern "Shushes" ringing in her ears. Her excitement at Damien's comment had got the better of her. *Quirky* is exactly what she usually looked for, and she told him so.

'Which is why,' she continued, 'I always like to come and check what new books you have in stock, just in case I find any snippets of new info. Course I do my research before I go, and ask locals when I'm there. But you never know where or when you're going to unearth that little gem of information. And when I uncover the gems, I like to go and check them out for myself and encourage my readers to do so, too. Providing they're worth seeing, of course. And they usually are.'

'Makes sense to me,' Damien said. 'It sounds like you make each trip a thorough adventure, rather than just a perfunctory visit. Good on you. What's your last name? I'll have to keep an eye out for your articles in ...' He paused for a second, then said, 'Actually, do you write for books, magazines, newspapers or websites?'

Annalise laughed.

'My last name is Berger. And, all of the above. I'm freelance, so theoretically anyone who will pay me.'

Damien nodded. 'I hear ya. So what time is your flight?'

Annalise looked at her watch. 'Oh, I have about an hour yet. Why?'

'I'm due a break. Wanna go and grab a drink and a snack? I'd love to hear more about your travels.'

'Um, sure.' She sure hadn't been expecting that, but she was more than happy to spend more time chatting with him.

Damien went to let his colleague know he was going for his break, then he and Annalise headed out of the bookshop.

'Well,' Damien said, glancing across at Annalise as they walked side by side, 'I guess you know this airport better than me, so where's the best place to go?'

Annalise laughed. 'There's not really that much choice, but I just fancy a muffin and a drink, so is the cafe OK?'

'Fine by me. Chocolate?'

'Huh?'

'A chocolate muffin?'

'I don't know yet. I'll see what's on offer. Why?' She resisted the urge to hide her stomach behind her hands. Did he think she looked like she ate a lot of chocolate?

'Oh, it's my first choice every time. I just wondered if you were a fellow chocoholic as well as bookworm and travel lover.'

Annalise grinned. Damien had obviously clocked on to the fact that they had a lot in common, too. She said nothing, the sound of her heels the only noise that came from either of them until they reached the cafe.

Moving towards the end of the mercifully short queue, Annalise instinctively started looking around at the tables to see if any were free, or if people looked like they were almost done. She was so engrossed in her task that she jumped when Damien's voice came from close behind her.

'Quick,' he said, his arm reaching over her shoulder and pointing. 'They're leaving. Go grab that table. What are you having?'

Damien's close proximity meant she could feel the heat of his body, as well as getting another whiff of that gorgeous scent he was wearing. She forced her response out of her mouth before he thought she was an indecisive weirdo.

'White coffee, two sugars, and a muffin please.' She started to edge towards the family vacating their table. She didn't want to dash right up and look like she was literally jumping into their seats. Although that's exactly what she was going to do.

'What flavour?' Damien asked while she was still in earshot.

'Chocolate!' she shot back over her shoulder as she moved quickly towards the now-empty table. She couldn't help grinning. She'd had no intention of having any flavour of muffin that wasn't chocolate. She'd just felt a little defensive when he'd assumed. But then he'd 'fessed up to being a chocoholic himself. That changed things.

It also made him even more fabulous. Intelligence, books, travel, chocolate; he ticked all the boxes, so far. And he was a cutie to boot.

She pulled out a chair and checked it for crumbs – or worse – before sitting down. Then she glanced back across the cafe towards Damien, who was just tucking his wallet back into his pocket. A strand of his hair had escaped from his hairband and he made the adorable tucking-behind-the-ears motion again before picking up the tray with their drinks and muffins. He looked straight at Annalise as he walked towards the table. When he saw she was looking, he glanced down at the chocolate muffins, back at her and wiggled his eyebrows, making her giggle.

She was still giggling as Damien put the tray on the table,

pulled out the chair opposite her, also checking it was clean, and sat down. He looked at her, an amused expression on his face, and the faintest hint of the dimple appearing in his cheek.

'Something amusing you, madam?'

'You know full well, sir.'

Damien laughed. 'Here, take your muffin before I eat them both.'

'You wouldn't deprive a fellow chocoholic from her fix now, would you? Especially since all I've got to look forward to in the next few hours is a crap airplane meal.'

Unloading the contents of the tray onto the table, he then propped it up against the table leg. Then he slid one of the muffin-laden plates towards her, as well as a napkin.

'You're right, of course. I would never deprive a lady.'

Annalise couldn't help but pick up the double entendre in his words. She sincerely doubted he'd meant anything by it, especially since it was a pretty lame play on words. He could undoubtedly do much better than that. The trouble was, Damien was sparking her brain as well as her body and making her read too much into what he said. And she was so out of touch that she had no idea if he liked her as more than a friend. The annoying thing was, if she was just trying to pick him up for a quick knee-trembler or one-nighter, she'd be pretty blatant about her intentions and know one way or another if he wanted her. But this was different. She liked him, and although she was definitely not averse to jumping his bones, she wanted more than that.

Annalise suddenly wished she could speak to her best friend, Tammy, and get her advice. Unfortunately, that wasn't an option. Tammy was in the military, and currently on a six-month tour of Afghanistan with only occasional contact by email. She had a pretty good handle on men and their minds – given she spent so much time around so many of them – but there was a good chance that even if Annalise emailed her, by the time she got a response, the moment would have passed. No, Annalise would have to deal with this one on her own.

'You OK?' Damien asked, interrupting her train of thought. 'You've gone all quiet. And you haven't even touched your muffin! I'd be happy to take it off your hands if you've lost your appetite.'

She playfully slapped the hand he'd reached across the table. 'Back off. This one's mine.'

Their eyes met, and Annalise felt her heart skip a beat at the intense look on his face. Particularly as she'd been expecting him to be grinning at their silly joke, rather than looking all serious. A couple of seconds passed, then Damien awkwardly dropped his gaze and became incredibly interested in his muffin. Annalise raised an eyebrow and reached for her own bundle of calorie-stuffed goodness and started to eat.

Now, she thought, that terrible double entendre was probably accidental, but that look definitely wasn't. Either he really wanted her muffin, or he liked her.

A little smile tugged at the corner of Annalise's mouth, then quickly died. Even if he did like her, what next? She didn't have the guts to ask him out. What if she'd got it totally wrong and he was just being friendly? What if he had a girlfriend? She was quite sure she'd die of embarrassment. Not literally, obviously, but still ... she went into that bookshop every time she left on a new trip, there was no way she'd be able to show her face in there again if he turned her down. And then where would she go? Oh, Tammy. What would you do?

'Are you sure you're all right?' Damien said, looking at her with concern. 'I'm not boring you, am I?'

'No!' she said, a little too forcefully, resulting in a few strange looks and frowns from people on nearby tables. She blushed and lowered her voice. 'Sorry, I mean no, of course not. I've just got a lot on my mind, with the trip and stuff. I can never relax properly when I know I've got a plane to catch. Even though I always get here in plenty of time, I'm always paranoid that somehow I'm not going to hear the gate number being announced or something, and end up being the one that holds up the plane. I hate being late. I'm sorry if I'm being weird.'

The words came out of her mouth with no hesitation, which made the lie completely convincing. Of course, it wasn't a total lie; she really did think and feel that way. But she couldn't exactly tell him the complete truth, could she? That she fancied the pants off him but was too shit scared to ask him out on a date. That would be the most humiliating conversation ever.

'Come on,' he said, 'just try and relax for a little while. Look at that information screen. Your flight's the fourth one down on the list, for a guess. Am I right?'

Annalise twisted around in her seat to look at the screen he was indicating. 'Yep, that's me.'

'Well then, you have a while to go. I promise faithfully to keep an eye on that screen and let you know the minute your gate number is announced. Deal?'

'Deal.'

They grinned at one another across the table and tucked into their muffins simultaneously. For a while they ate in companionable silence. Damien finished his snack first and announced his extreme appreciation before taking a sip of his drink and wiping his mouth thoroughly with his napkin.

Annalise couldn't resist. Washing down the remaining crumbs of her muffin with a sip of coffee, she swallowed, and said, 'You missed a bit.'

Damien's eyes widened with surprise. 'I did?' He swiped furiously at his face with a clean paper tissue, seemingly determined to remove the stray crumbs.

Annalise bit her inside lip to keep from laughing.

'Has it gone?' Damien said, moving his head from side to side so she could see the non-existent chocolate.

'Nope,' she said, barely suppressing her laughter. 'It's

still there.'

'Show me, please. I can't walk about looking like this.'

You look pretty fine to me, Annalise thought. She reached out and grabbed his wrist to direct him to the imaginary mess on his face. As their skin made contact, Damien looked her in the eye, waiting for her to move. Annalise froze. His intense gaze was making her heart thump almost painfully, and sending hormones racing through her body. She felt her pussy leaking juices onto the gusset of her thong, and could barely believe what was happening.

What on earth was it about this man that was making her react this way? They'd done nothing even *remotely* sexual and yet she was getting so horny that if he suggested a trip to the toilets, or even the back room of the bookshop she'd say yes in a heartbeat.

Not that he would, of course. He was a nice guy, not someone who was likely to suggest seedy encounters in toilets or back rooms. But it didn't stop her wanting to fuck him.

Suddenly realising that she was still gripping his wrist, Annalise snatched her hand away before Damien began to consider filing a restraining order. Her movement snapped them both out of their "weird moment" and Damien dabbed absentmindedly at his lips a couple more times before dropping the napkin on the table, the non-existent smudge on his face seemingly forgotten.

This time the silence wasn't companionable. It was downright awkward. They sipped at their drinks, glancing at each other occasionally before looking away. Annalise could have screamed with frustration. They were behaving like immature teenagers. The only consolation Annalise took from their furtive idiocy was the fact that it wouldn't be happening if there wasn't something between them. It was a tiny consolation, granted, but it made her feel a bit better and spurred her on to rescue their conversation before things became so strained they gave up on one another as a lost cause.

'So ...' Annalise said, a little too brightly, 'tell me more about yourself. I only know the bare minimum, and I don't usually have coffee and chocolate muffins with strange guys.'

Annalise noticed Damien's shoulders sag with relief at the conversational lifeline she'd thrown.

'Who are you calling strange?' His dimple appeared again as he smiled, and Annalise's instant reaction was to smile back. Her heart did a flip-flop. She had a feeling that his smile would always have that effect on her. Mercifully, Damien's silly joke had caused the weird atmosphere to evaporate, and he started to talk. He told her about himself, his life, his hobbies; it was as if the awkwardness had never existed.

Annalise had no idea how long they'd been sitting laughing and exchanging anecdotes, until suddenly Damien's gaze moved away from her and focussed on something in the distance. His expression changed, and sent a lump of panic into Annalise's throat.

'Oh fuck, am I late?' She necked the remainder of her – almost cold – coffee, stood up and started gathering her things together hastily.

'No, no, not yet,' Damien said. 'It's the second call for your gate. I obviously missed the first one. I'm so sorry. But they're not calling your name yet, so it's all good.'

'Shit,' Annalise said, scrambling to open her bag and retrieve her purse. 'I owe you for the coffee and muffin.'

Standing, Damien put his hand over hers. 'Don't worry about it, consider it my treat.'

Glancing over at the information screen, the blinking letters beside her flight sent a fresh rush of panic coursing through her. 'I'm so sorry Damien, I have to run.'

'I know, I know. Just go. Do you have everything?'

Looking around wildly, Annalise nodded.

'I do.' She was torn. There was so much she wanted to say. They hadn't exchanged numbers, emails or anything. Once they'd started talking again, there hadn't been a pause until Damien had happened to check the information screen. And thank God he had.

'I really have to go. I'll catch up with you later, yeah? Next muffin's on me.'

Damien smiled. 'Looking forward to it. Now go.'

Pausing momentarily, Annalise wondered whether to kiss him goodbye or not. Not a full on kiss, of course, but just a peck. It was such a cliché, but she knew she'd kick herself if she didn't. Oh, what the hell.

She pressed a quick kiss to his cheek, causing them both to blush. Then she said quietly, 'See you soon.'

Turning away from Damien, she walked as fast as she reasonably could in heels in the direction of her departure gate. She only hoped her last words were true.

Mentally shaking herself, she thought, of course you'll see him soon, you idiot. You're at this damn airport all the time. And he works here. Stop being such a wuss. It'll work out.

She joined the back of the queue of passengers boarding the flight and retrieved her passport and boarding card from her bag. Heaving a sigh of relief, she told herself that just because she was the last passenger to board, didn't mean she was late. She wasn't holding up the plane. Everything was fine.

Finally, she settled into her window seat – after the terrible embarrassment of having to ask people to move so she could sit down – and shucked off her shoes. She retrieved her Kindle from her bag and put it on her lap, before stuffing the bag under the seat in front of her.

As an image of Damien's face and intense green eyes flashed through her mind, Annalise thanked her lucky stars that she'd loaded her Kindle with several new books before leaving for this trip. It was going to be a long flight.

Chapter Three

EMERGING FROM THE TAXI, Annalise quickly slipped her sunglasses down from where they'd been perched on her head into their rightful position. It was late in the day so it wasn't too hot, but it sure was sunny. She turned to where the taxi driver was retrieving her bag from the boot of the car. He slammed the lid then began happily walking towards the front doors of the hotel with her bag.

'It's OK,' she said, waving to get his attention, 'I can carry it. It's fine, honestly.'

She might as well have been talking to the wall. The man simply kept smiling and said, 'Is no problem. Really.'

Annalise stopped herself from rolling her eyes. He was only being polite, after all. She went to most places alone, and was used to doing things for herself. She wasn't being ungrateful. She followed the driver without another word until they were in front of the reception desk, where he carefully deposited her bag on the floor. Annalise crouched down to reach inside for her purse, where she pulled out a note and handed it to the driver.

His eyes widened as he took it, and he said, 'I get you change.'

'No,' Annalise replied, gently. 'Keep the change. Thank you.'

He opened his mouth to protest, but a look and a raised eyebrow from Annalise stopped him. 'Thank you, Miss. Have a nice trip. I maybe see you when you go home?'

'Maybe.' Annalise grinned. She took so many trips to foreign countries a year, and yet she still couldn't get used to the mannerisms and friendliness. Back home, neighbours passed in the street without speaking. She gave the driver a wave as he left, then turned to the reception desk ready to check in. She was greeted by another smiling face. It was infectious, and she found her mood lifting. She wasn't feeling grumpy, as such, it was just that even the short flight she'd just taken had made her feel travel weary. Now she was starting to perk up a little and she genuinely felt happy that she was here. Yes, it was work – despite all her mother's comments to the contrary – but she loved it. She couldn't relax in the same way she did when on holiday, as she was always on the lookout for things to include in her articles, but it certainly wasn't all bad.

It would be better if Damien were here, though. The thought entered her head completely out of the blue. Once there, however, she couldn't seem to get rid of it. She shoved it to the back of her mind as she went through the hotel's check-in process, then thanked the receptionist and made to leave for her room. Before she could pick up her bag, an enthusiastic young bellhop had grabbed it and was walking in front of her to call the lift. Annalise gritted her teeth. It looked as though she'd have to wait a little longer to be alone with her thoughts.

Sliding the plastic card into the slot in the door, she heaved a sigh of relief when the light flashed green. These things could be so temperamental, but she'd obviously got the knack of it over the years. She relieved the bellhop of her bag, tipped him and practically ran into her room, shutting and locking the door behind her.

Ahh. It was so nice to be alone at last. Now, where was she? Oh yes, Damien had popped into her head at the most unexpected moment. Annalise looked at her watch. It was hard to believe they'd only met a few hours ago, and yet she'd struggled to concentrate on her book on the flight because she was thinking about him, and now here he was again, invading her thoughts. Bloody man.

She wondered if he was thinking of her too. She hoped so. Then, determined not to torture herself with questions she couldn't possibly answer, Annalise decided to unpack her bags, find her clean clothes and take a shower. Then she'd take her laptop down to the bar and get some work done.

An hour or so later, she was feeling much cleaner and more invigorated as she tucked her laptop under her arm and headed down to the hotel bar. All the rooms had WiFi, but how was she meant to soak up the atmosphere of the place if she was holed up by herself? Plus, having had a little alone time, she was ready to face the world and socialise with people again. Or at least be around them, anyway.

Her flip-flops slapped against the marble floor as Annalise entered the bar, effectively announcing her arrival. It was fairly quiet, but the few people who'd glanced up when she walked in gave polite nods and smiles, which she returned. Looking towards the bar, Annalise could see that the smartly-dressed member of staff behind it was already giving her his undivided attention, and she hadn't got within ten paces of the bar yet.

'Hi,' she said, checking the bar top for any spills before carefully putting her laptop down. 'Can I get a vodka and Red Bull, please?'

Annalise gave her room number and waited as the barman made her drink. When he turned back and put her drink down in front of her, she thanked him and made to go and sit down at one of the tables. She couldn't work at the bar; she had her back to the room, and past experience told her that even if she said she was working, her presence there still invited conversation from the people working behind it.

'Miss?' Annalise felt her heart sink as her escape was halted. 'You need the WiFi?'

He looked pointedly at her laptop.

'Um, yes.'

'One moment.' He went through a door which looked as

though it led into a back office and came back shortly afterwards with a leaflet in his hand. Handing it to her, he said, 'Information is here how to use the WiFi.'

'Thank you.' She looked at his name badge, 'Andre. I'd forgotten about that.'

He inclined his head. 'No problem.'

His use of English slang made her smile, and she was still grinning as she picked up her laptop and drink and made her way to a table at the back of the room. She sat with the rest of the room to her right, a window to her left and the bar in front, and opened up her laptop. Switching it on and entering her password, Annalise then took a sip of her drink and gazed out of the window while she waited for the machine to do its thing.

It was dark outside now, so she couldn't see much, only what was illuminated by the moon and the lights dotted around the complex. She picked up the shimmer of the pool, the nets of the tennis court, and the lights of what she suspected was a restaurant or another bar on the other side of the pool. Before she had time to contemplate it, a ping from her computer announced it was ready to go. Grabbing the leaflet that Andre had given her, Annalise followed the instructions and heaved a sigh of relief when the WiFi symbol came up in her taskbar. She was online.

A check of her emails proved uninteresting, as did her Facebook account. Unless ...

Annalise typed his name into the search box and hit enter. The WiFi wasn't particularly speedy, so after a short wait the page loaded up, and there he was! She clicked on his photograph and grinned like an idiot as his page came up. It looked as though he'd set most of his controls to private as she couldn't see much beyond his name and photo, but it was enough. She moved the cursor until it was over the "Add Friend" button. She went to click, then hesitated.

Was it a bit stalkerish? Would he think it was weird that

she was abroad for work, yet she'd gone on to Facebook and found him and requested him as a friend just a few short hours after they'd met?

Annalise sighed and typed another URL into the browser, removing the temptation. And besides, Google Maps always distracted her. She'd use it to have a look at what was nearby, then do more research to see which places looked worth a visit.

Annalise sipped her drink absentmindedly as she surfed the web. A little while later, she exclaimed as she realised her glass was empty. Picking it up, she stood ready to go back to the bar for a refill. Looking around, she felt confident that nobody in the room was going to do a runner with her laptop. She'd known that already, really. This was a pretty upmarket establishment. People who stayed here could definitely afford their own laptops, if they wanted them.

Mooching back up to where Andre stood polishing glasses with his back to her, she cleared her throat. He turned and beamed at her.

'Hello again. Would you like another?'

'No, can I have coke instead of Red Bull this time please, Andre? I don't want to be up all night.'

It was only when Andre raised his eyebrows and gave a wicked grin that she realised her gaffe. Ah well, it was too late to take it back now, so she said nothing, hoping that he wouldn't notice the blush that she felt coming to her cheeks. Andre dumped her dirty glass in the dishwasher and got her a clean one, then mixed her new drink. He slid it gently across to her, then leaned on his elbows on the bar and gave her a quizzical look.

'How is your work going, Miss? Only I see you smile, then I see you frown at the screen.'

'Oh,' she said, a little embarrassed that he'd been watching her. She knew she pulled faces when she was concentrating, but she was normally alone or nobody was taking any notice, so it didn't matter. 'It's going OK. I've just been looking at things to do around here.'

'That is your work? What is your job?'

'I'm a writer,' she replied. She'd had this conversation with bar staff, bellhops, waiters and gym managers the world over, so the simplified explanation came out without much thought. 'I visit places then write articles about them. The hotels, the area, the beaches, the entertainment, the tourist attractions...'

She tailed off. Andre was nodded enthusiastically, so she'd obviously got her point across. Either that or he was bored now and wanted her to shut up. Either way, his next words surprised her.

'Do you like castelos ... um ... castles? There is one nearby.'

'I love castles!' Annalise replied delightedly. Then, confused, she asked, 'Where is it? Only it didn't come up on Google Maps.'

It couldn't very well be new, could it? Unless castles were all the rage in new developments these days.

Andre named a village a short distance away. 'You have heard of it?'

Annalise nodded. She'd been scouring the map long enough to have a pretty good working knowledge of the area.

'It is near there. But in the hills. You know, good position for ... um ... fighting.'

He waved his right arm around and wiggled his hips, mimicking the movements you'd make if you were sword fighting.

Annalise laughed. 'You mean a good strategic position?'

He clapped his hands. 'Yes! I did not know the words.'

'Brilliant, thank you, Andre. I think I will go there first tomorrow, before it gets too hot.'

'How will you get there? There are no buses, and taxi will be expensive.'

'Oh,' she replied, desperate to get away and do some more research on the internet now she'd found a quirky gem for her article, 'I'm going to hire a car in the morning.'

'No need,' he said, waving his hands around, then pressing one to his chest, 'I take you. I know the area, and the castle. I am tour guide sometimes, for my brother's company. And I am not working here until the evening tomorrow.'

'Really?' Annalise wasn't as surprised by his offer as she ought to be. The whole "travelling the world, experiencing different cultures" thing meant that it was an offer she'd received on more than one occasion. When she first started working as a travel writer, it freaked her out, as she was convinced that the guys were up to no good. Back home you'd probably think a total stranger offering to take you somewhere was a serial killer or rapist. But she'd come to realise that they were genuine, selfless offers. For the most part she turned them down, preferring to do her own thing. She'd made exceptions for some of the better-looking guys, but they'd rarely made it to the final destination, ending up fucking in some random place then running out of time before they had to be elsewhere.

Annalise smiled. She'd had some fun on those random, horny road-trips. Not to mention some totally hot sex. Plus, after the day she'd had, her body was telling her she was long overdue for some more, and she could do much worse than Andre. Also, unless he was bullshitting her, it would appear he actually knew stuff about the local area that would be useful. He'd almost be doing her job for her.

Andre grinned back at her, clearly taking the gesture as consent. 'Yes? What time shall I come?'

Annalise almost snorted with laughter, but managed to turn it into a cough. The mixture of talking to people who didn't speak English as their first language and her dirty mind was not a good one. Her brain often twisted their words into ones they didn't mean, leaving her giggling like a teenage boy on the inside, while trying to remain cool and collected on the outside. It didn't always work. Luckily, Andre bought it.

They chatted a little longer, making arrangements for the following day. By the time they'd sorted it, Annalise's drink was down to the dregs. She downed the remains and Andre made her another one before she went back to the table, and her laptop.

The clock in the corner of the screen, which she knew was right as there was no time difference between home and here, told her that it was getting pretty late. Annalise wasn't particularly tired – the Red Bull in her first vodka had seen to that – so she decided to take her time finishing her drink, and then head back upstairs. If she still wasn't sleepy, she could read for a little while before getting into bed. Nodding to herself, she tapped at the laptop's trackerpad to bring the screen back up.

As the machine hummed back into life and brought up her browser window, Annalise moved the mouse cursor up to the "Home" button. However, the drinks she'd had, coupled with the small amount of food she'd eaten that day meant that she wasn't quite as dexterous as usual. She accidentally hit the "Back" button instead, bringing up Damien's Facebook profile again. She sighed. There he was again. He was thousands of miles away and yet he still kept appearing in front of her. She was about to attempt clicking the "Home" button as she'd originally intended, but something stopped her.

Maybe it was the alcohol making her bold – or stupid – but before she could talk herself out of it again, Annalise had clicked to request Damien as a friend. She decided to send a little message along with her request, just to make it seem a little more casual.

Hi Damien. Good to meet you earlier. Have arrived safely, am just heading to bed. Just wanted to send a quick message

to say sorry for dashing off like that, and thanks for the
coffee and muffin. They're on me next time.
Take care, Annalise

She hit send quickly, before she had time to read and re-read what she'd written. She knew if she did, she'd just agonise over what she'd said in case she'd been too forward, too casual, too clingy ... whatever. She may be in her mid 30s, but it sure didn't stop her acting like a lovesick teenager from time to time. Probably because she had about the same amount of experience at relationships.

Shaking her head, Annalise got rid of the Facebook window and pulled up Google. She typed in the name of the castle she and Andre were going to visit the following day. There were only a couple of links available, but she followed them anyway, gleaning what she could. It certainly looked like an interesting place and hopefully Andre's insider knowledge would give her some tasty titbits to include in her article, too.

A little while later, having exhausted the small amount of information she'd found online, Annalise shut down the laptop. Finishing her drink, she picked up her laptop and glass and returned to the bar. Putting her glass down, she gave a little wave to Andre who was serving someone else. He saw her out of the corner of his eye, and without stopping what he was doing, he yelled to her, 'I will see you tomorrow. Sleep well.'

Annalise smiled tightly and gave a curt nod, and then nodded politely at the customer Andre had been serving, who was now looking at her strangely. She wished he hadn't shouted out like that. Now everyone would think she was some woman who went around picking up male bar staff in hotels. Of course, that was exactly what she did, sometimes, but she was damn subtle about it.

Oh well, there was nothing to be done about it now. She left without a backward glance and headed up to her room.

Chapter Four

THE FOLLOWING MORNING ANNALISE woke up before her alarm went off, which annoyed her immensely. She and Andre had arranged a time which wasn't too early, due to his late shift at work, so she could have had a little extra sleep. But once she was awake, she was awake. She rolled over on the sumptuous double bed and grabbed her phone from the bedside table. 7.15 a.m. She put the phone down, clambered out of bed and walked into the bathroom, flicking on the kettle on the dresser as she passed.

By the time she'd done in the bathroom, the water had almost boiled. Tipping a sachet of cappuccino-flavoured powder into a mug, Annalise waited for the kettle to click, announcing its job was done, before pouring the water. Stirring the drink, she then left it to cool for a little while before throwing on some clothes. She'd shower before going out with Andre, but for now she was going to chill out on her balcony for a little while.

Fortunately for Annalise, her room faced east so when she pulled open the curtains, the rising sun shone through the sliding glass doors on to her. Undoing the catch, she slid the panel open, moved out onto the balcony and arranged the table and a chair so she had the best view across the hotel complex. Then she dashed back inside to grab her cappuccino and laptop, which she'd put on charge when she got back to the room last night. She'd check her emails and the morning news from the comfort of her backside before getting ready for her day out with Andre.

Annalise grabbed her cappuccino and leaned against the

wall of the balcony, sipping idly at the drink as she waited for the laptop to boot up. She gazed out at the world below, which was quiet at this time of the morning. There was only a handful of people around, and as far as Annalise could tell, they were all staff. They were watering the plants, emptying bins and generally making the place as perfect as could be for the patrons. Nice, but not particularly interesting. She was just about to turn back to the laptop and see if she could find something more entertaining to look at, when she caught a movement out of the corner of her eye. It wasn't on the ground floor, where she'd seen the staff, but much higher up. Perhaps the fourth or fifth storey of the building.

Regardless of the storey, the view was a damn sight more interesting than plants being watered. From her vantage point, she had the perfect view of what could only be described as the perfect arse. It belonged to a man who was doing what she'd been doing only seconds ago; leaning on the balcony and watching the world go by. Unlike him, though, she'd been fully clothed.

Not that she was complaining. He certainly had the body for wandering around in the buff. In profile, he looked good enough to eat. He was tall, dark-haired and had the muscular, bronzed body of a sun-worshipper. He probably didn't have two brain cells to rub together, but Annalise wasn't bothered. She wasn't going to marry the guy, just have a good look at what he was showing off. And he *had* to be showing off, she decided. It was bloody obvious; if you're going to walk around naked on a balcony, then surely you'd know that people on the floors above will be able to see you. He obviously didn't care, so she wasn't going to feel guilty about having a good look.

She didn't have the opportunity to do much more totty-watching, unfortunately, as the man – like her – must have decided there wasn't really much entertainment going on this early in the morning. He turned away from the balcony wall, giving Annalise a flash of his rather impressive cock, before heading inside.

Annalise was frozen for a few seconds, hardly believing what she'd just seen. A shirtless man was one thing – they were two-a-penny when abroad – but completely naked? His cock, despite its flaccid state, had still made her raise her eyebrows. Sniggering to herself, Annalise decided that even if Mr Naked *was* as dumb as a box of rocks he'd have no trouble attracting the ladies looking like that. He'd have no trouble keeping them, either, especially if he was a grower rather than a shower.

Still smiling, Annalise shook her head and seated herself in front of the laptop. She'd had her quota of excitement for the morning; it was now time to see what was happening in the rest of the world. Her emails turned up nothing of interest or importance, which wasn't surprising. Annalise was organised enough that she got all urgent tasks completed before jetting off somewhere, just in case she wasn't reachable whilst there.

The news was barely more stimulating. It was all stocks and shares, banking crises, politics and bad news. Dull. Annalise slumped in her chair, thinking she may as well finish her cappuccino and go and have a shower. She could always mooch around downstairs and make some notes on the hotel while she waited for Andre. She was just about to shut down the laptop when she remembered something. Damien. Oh God, she'd "friend requested" him on Facebook last night!

Hurriedly she typed in the URL and waited for it to load. Come on, bloody WiFi! Why are you so slow? Eventually her homepage came up and she logged in. And waited, again. Soon she was looking at a list of what her "friends" had been up to, what they'd been eating, where they'd checked in and all manner of boring twaddle. There was only one thing she was really interested in, and she wasn't going to find it in the News Feed. She could see she had no messages, so he obviously hadn't replied to her little note.

Perhaps he'd just accepted her as a friend and left it at that.

Typing in his name and hitting "search" brought up his page again, but unfortunately it was much the same as last night. She could only see the bare essentials, which meant ... her gaze strayed to the button. Damn. It still said 'Friend Requested' which meant he hadn't accepted her! He obviously thought she had been a little too enthusiastic and was now avoiding her, virtually, of course. Or, she thought, grateful that the more rational side of her brain had kicked in, he may not have been on Facebook. Not everyone checks it every day, you know.

Nodding, she logged out of the website and powered down the computer. Her rational mind was correct, of course. It usually was. Everything was just fine, so she'd leave it at that and get on with her day. Which, looking up at the sky, was going to be a beautiful one. She made a mental note to plaster on some sun cream before she went out to meet Andre. Moving her laptop and her now-empty mug back into her hotel room, she put them down and went back to shut and lock the balcony door. Pulling the curtains closed – she may be on the sixth floor but she sure as hell wasn't taking a chance on any opportunistic peeping Toms – Annalise undressed and dropped her clothes onto a chair before heading for the bathroom.

She pulled the door shut behind her and wasted no time in switching on the shower, waiting for the water to warm up and jumping in. It was over a bath and so she had plenty of room to stretch out and wash. She hated those tiny little cubicles where she could barely bend her arms enough to wash her hair. Retrieving the posh shampoo from the shelf beside her, she squeezed a generous amount into her other hand and put the bottle back. Then she tilted her head back under the spray to get her blonde hair nice and wet, leaving it a couple of seconds before smearing the gloopy liquid into her locks. She scrubbed her scalp nice and hard, sometimes finding it an effective way of waking her up and getting the old grey matter working. Not to mention it felt damn good.

This morning, at least, her plan was working. Her brain was soon firing on all synapses. The trouble was those synapses were bringing forth the most inappropriate and unwanted thoughts. First, Annalise found herself daydreaming about the naked guy on the balcony as she conditioned and rinsed her hair. Having gone through an internal debate as to whether he *was* a grower or a shower – which remained unresolved – her thoughts then strayed to her earlier foray on Facebook. Which, inevitably, made her think of Damien.

She was sure now that he wasn't ignoring or avoiding her or anything unpleasant like that, so she quit obsessing about it. Instead, she found herself thinking about what Damien would look like naked. Nothing like Mr Naked, she was sure. He was shorter, with crazy curly hair and a slim frame, for starters. She was glad. Annalise would rather have Damien with his intense green stare, his dimple and his love of books, travel and chocolate than a tanned gym freak.

Annalise smiled. His stare really *was* intense. The way he'd looked at her over that table yesterday ... if she didn't know any better she'd have believed he was having some seriously naughty thoughts. Not that she minded. God knows she'd been thinking about him enough.

A sudden laugh bubbled up out of her throat as she remembered the way she'd teased him about having chocolate on his face. He'd been so determined to wipe it off that he hadn't noticed the way she'd been desperately trying not to laugh. She'd have to 'fess up to him at some point. She was sure he'd find it as funny as she did. As her mind replayed his actions, she recalled how nice his hands were, and wondered how those long slim fingers would feel playing over her naked flesh.

Annalise stroked her hands down her body, moving more slowly and firmly over the tips of her breasts before skimming down her gently rounded stomach and towards the juncture of her thighs. As her left hand remained on her mound, stroking her perfectly groomed landing strip, her right hand slipped lower and delved between her legs. Unsurprisingly, she was a little wet, and not just from the shower.

Throwing herself wholeheartedly into the fantasy, Annalise imagined it was Damien gently parting her pussy lips; Damien who was stroking the sensitive flesh; Damien who was ... *Oooh.* Annalise's fingers played over her rapidly swelling clit, teasing and stroking it the way she knew was guaranteed to bring her to a quick and satisfying orgasm.

And orgasm she did. Slamming her free hand against the wall to steady herself, Annalise wailed her release, belatedly hoping the sound of the shower would drown out the sounds she was making. As her pussy clenched wildly around nothing, Annalise wished she had a hard cock up there, pumping to its own climax inside her. A hard body steadying her and stroking her hair as she came down from her orgasm. She missed that.

Pulling her hand from between her thighs and reaching for the shower gel, Annalise came to the conclusion that Damien or no Damien, she needed to get laid, and soon. She may like visiting churches and religious buildings on her travels to admire their architecture, but she was certainly no nun!

Chapter Five

ANNALISE WAS TAPPING HER foot, huffily thinking she'd been stood up and wondering where the nearest car hire place was, when a car pulled up beside her and Andre waved at her from the driver's seat. The vehicle was no Mercedes, but then she hadn't been expecting it to be. As long as it got her from A to B and back again, she didn't care. Opening the car door and getting in, she gave him a wry smile, then turned to put her bag on the back seat.

'I'm sorry, Annalise. I am a little bit late.' *No shit, Sherlock.* 'But my mother, she asked me to do something for her. I tell her I am going out, but ...' He shrugged. 'I will drive fast to make up for it!'

'No, you won't!' she exclaimed, instinctively reaching for her seatbelt and clipping it into place. 'It's fine. We have ages. Until we have to be back here for your shift tonight, right?'

'Right,' he replied, putting the car into gear. 'You are ready?'

'I'm ready, Andre. Let's go.'

He pulled away from the kerb and out into the traffic. They motored along in silence for a while, and Annalise watched the world go by, making mental notes about the bars, cafes and shops that they passed. She'd come back and explore the more generic places later or tomorrow. But for now, it was all about the quirky. About the gem.

She grinned.

'You are happy for today, Annalise?' Andre asked, not taking his eyes off the road. She had no idea if he normally drove this carefully and attentively, or whether it was for her benefit. Either way, she much preferred it to the motoring craziness that she normally experienced in foreign countries like this.

'I am, Andre. Thank you for offering to be my tour guide for the day. I really appreciate it.'

'It is OK,' he replied. 'It is better than caring for my mother, and brothers and sisters!'

He shrugged again, and Annalise couldn't help but ask the question that had been bugging her since their conversation the previous evening.

'Don't you have a girlfriend, or a wife, Andre?'

He glanced at her then, a tiny smile tugging at his lips. Then he looked back at the road ahead and said, 'No girlfriend or wife. My family, they keep me so busy I do not have time for women. The only ones I meet are at work. And they are mostly customers.'

Annalise got the impression it was a bit of a sore point, so she didn't pry any further. If he wanted to tell her, he would.

'What about you, Annalise? Do you have boyfriend or husband?'

'No. A little bit like you, Andre, I am too busy for men.' She tried not to think too much about how pathetic that sounded. Too busy for a love life, how sad was that?

Well, she thought, I promised myself I would try and rectify that situation, and I am. I met Damien and I like him. I'm just ...

What *was* she doing, exactly? They'd hit it off and had a chat and a coffee together. That didn't mean they were going to skip off into the sunset together.

Maybe not. But I'm going to give it a bloody good go. In the meantime ...

She looked across at Andre. She hadn't really noticed last night – she put it down to tiredness – but he *was* cute. He had cropped dark hair, and gorgeous brown eyes. He wore a white T-shirt which set off his olive skin to perfection, and black shorts. He also hadn't yet shaved, so a day's worth of stubble graced his jaw. He didn't look rough and ready, exactly, but he also didn't look like the mummy's boy he so clearly was.

He hadn't replied to her last statement. She could understand why. After all, what precisely could he say? He was in the same boat as her, so he could appreciate how life got in the way of ... well, life.

Refusing to let her thoughts continue wandering down that long and maudlin road, Annalise steered the topic of conversation on to a much safer track.

'So!' she said brightly, and a little too loudly, startling Andre. 'How long will it take us to get to the castle?'

'Not long now. Perhaps ten minutes?'

'Cool. I can't wait.'

He smiled, and Annalise noticed how his smile made his already handsome face very attractive indeed. She decided that she was definitely going to make a play for Andre, if he'd have her. It had been way too long since she'd last had sex, and if she and Damien actually got it together then it would be nice to get back into practice beforehand.

Who was she kidding? Get back into practice? Whatever! Andre was hot and single, she was horny and single. No more bullshit about life getting in the way of life. She was going to take each opportunity as it came, starting now. The poor guy wouldn't know what hit him.

Soon, they arrived at their destination. Andre had been right, she'd have really struggled to get here using public transport, and given the lack of road signs she may not have found it at all, even by car. Nevertheless, here they were and as Andre pulled into the car park – if you could call the dusty open area that – Annalise asked, 'Where is everyone? Are we early?'

He parked the car and cut the engine. Turning to smile at her, he replied, 'No. The castillo is open all day, it is just that not many people visit. Perhaps your article will make more people visit soon.'

'I hope so, Andre. It certainly looks like this is a damn cool place that's been seriously overlooked.'

Grabbing her bag, Annalise got out of the car and walked across the car park to the front entrance of the castle with Andre in close pursuit. Almost immediately, her imagination started to run away with her. She thought about what the place would have been like in its heyday, how the people would have lived, what they would have done for entertainment ...

A couple of hours later, and Annalise had lots of photos on her camera, as well as several pages full of notes. Some were her own observations, but the majority were things that Andre had told her about the place as they made their way around it. She was delighted. This article was almost going to write itself.

They sat down on a bench on the edge of the property which had a lovely view across the surrounding countryside. Annalise sighed happily and enjoyed the feel of the sun warming her skin as she flipped through her notebook, skimming through what she'd written. When she'd finished, she shut the book with a satisfied nod and put it in her bag.

'You have what you need, Annalise? Was my information good?'

'Andre, it was brilliant! This article will write itself.'

Andre frowned, and Annalise realised he had no idea that she was using a colloquialism. She also had no idea how she would be able to explain its meaning. Instead, she settled for shuffling along the bench, flinging her arms around him and pulling him in for a hug.

She pulled back and said, 'Yes, you've been very helpful. I'm so grateful, thank you.'

A glance at Andre's face told Annalise that something was making him feel uncomfortable. She wondered if she'd gone too far with the hug – some people don't like to be touched, after all – when she spotted him glance down at where their bodies still touched. When she had disentangled from their embrace, she hadn't moved very far, and her left breast was pressed against his arm. It wasn't as though they were skin to skin – though her sundress wasn't exactly demure – but it was enough to cause a pink twinge to highlight Andre's cheeks. Bless him.

Despite his obvious embarrassment, he didn't move. If it was bothering him that much, surely he would have? There was room enough on the bench for him to shuffle away if he really wanted to. Annalise took that to mean he *didn't* really want to.

She leaned further into him, squashing her soft breast more tightly against his arm, and looked into his eyes. He still looked a little uncomfortable, but the longer he gazed back at her, the more his expression changed from one of discomfort to one of lust.

Reaching up to stroke his cheek, Annalise said, 'It's a real shame you don't have a girlfriend, Andre. You're a lovely guy, and very good looking.'

He said nothing, merely dropping his gaze from her face, where it alighted on the next area of significant interest. He stared at her breasts, barely covered by the neckline of her dress, for a few seconds before looking at her face once more.

'You are very beautiful, Annalise.'

Dropping her hand from his face, Annalise thought about kissing him – and more. What she'd said had been absolutely spot on, he *was* very good looking, and a bit of naughty fun under the Portuguese sun would be nice, but...

But what? What happened to taking each opportunity as it comes?

Sighing, Annalise stood up and retrieved her bag from the ground.

'What is the matter, Annalise? Did I say something wrong?'

She turned to him, shaking her head. 'No, you didn't, Andre. I'm sorry. I'm attracted to you, but I can't do anything about it.'

Andre stood, tugging his T-shirt down over what Annalise suspected was a now-waning erection. 'O ... K,' he said, hesitantly, 'you are sure I didn't do something wrong? You said you don't have a boyfriend.'

Annalise smiled at him. She'd made the poor guy paranoid now, which was certainly not what she'd intended. She was sorry she'd even hugged him now. After all, she was no prick tease.

'I don't, Andre,' she said softly. 'But there is someone I like very much. I don't know if he likes me, but I intend to find out.'

She started walking slowly back towards the castle and the car park. Andre stayed by her side.

'I understand,' he said.

After a pause, he continued, 'He is a very lucky man, to have a woman like you. If he doesn't like you, he is crazy! Then you come back and see me, eh?'

His wide grin told Annalise he had no hard feelings towards her, and she heaved a sigh of relief.

'Of course,' she replied, smiling back, 'you will be first on my list!'

They walked in silence back to the car and got in. They didn't say much on the journey back to the hotel, and she was relieved that Andre didn't push it. There wasn't really very much she could say, other than what she'd told him already.

Leaning her head against the window, she zoned out from the scenery that flashed past and wondered what on earth she was going to do about Damien. If he didn't respond to her Facebook message, then nothing, she guessed. She'd just have to suck it up and move on.

But if he did ...

She was still thinking about how and when she could see

183

Damien again, when she became vaguely aware that the car had stopped and that Andre was talking to her.

'Annalise? We are here.'

'Huh? Oh, sorry. I was miles away.' She realised they were in the underground car park of the hotel.

He smiled and raised an eyebrow. 'Thinking of your man?'

Feeling colour rush to her cheeks, Annalise murmured, 'I was, actually.'

'You must tell him,' Andre said decisively. 'Love is very important. Is not a game.'

His words and tone of voice made Annalise suspect there was more to his singledom than he was letting on, but she didn't mention it. She'd just knocked the guy back; she couldn't exactly start pumping him for details on his past love life. She just leaned across the car, dropped a kiss on his cheek, and said, 'Thank you. I will. See you later.'

Then she got out of the car and made her way to the lift that would take her upstairs, her mind full of Andre's words. He was right, of course. Love *wasn't* a game, so sooner or later she'd have to stop playing chicken.

Chapter Six

EXHAUSTED, ANNALISE FLOPPED ONTO the bed. After the crazy day she'd had, all she wanted to do was curl up and have a nap. However, she and Andre had spent longer at the castle than she'd expected, so she was a bit behind her self-imposed schedule. She'd planned to get back earlier, sort out the results of her day's work then go for a nice swim in the pool before showering and heading out for dinner and to check out the local nightlife.

Sighing, Annalise realised that wasn't going to happen. Not today, anyway. She shuffled off the bed and retrieved her laptop from the table and her notebook from her bag. She needed to type up her notes while they still made sense. Slumping back onto the bed, she settled the machine on her lap and booted it up.

Grabbing the notebook, she flicked to the first page of her notes for the day and skim-read the words while she waited for her laptop to ping its readiness. Then she opened up her emails and glanced through her inbox to see if there was anything of importance. A couple of messages stood out so she read them, then composed and sent the appropriate replies. Her inbox reappeared. It was only then that she noticed the email she'd received from Facebook. She usually didn't take too much notice of them – she really should get around to configuring her settings so they didn't send her the damn messages in the first place – but this one had piqued her interest.

She'd received a message from Damien Whittaker. Her heart rate increased as she quickly clicked on the email link and logged into the social networking site. Then a sudden sinking feeling hit her stomach. What if his message was dismissive, coolly polite, or worse; a simple "Hi"? Shaking her head, she mentally scolded herself. She'd never know until she read it.

Hi Annalise! Just logged into Facebook and saw your name pop up. Sorry it's taken so long to get back to you, I never check this bloody account. It's mostly people from school that I don't particularly want to talk to, so receiving your friend request and note was a welcome change!

Glad you caught your flight OK and arrived in one piece. Hope work is going OK.

Look forward to the free coffee and muffin ;)
See you soon, Damien

Annalise let out a tiny squeal of excitement. Then she read through the message another couple of times before satisfying herself that it was 100 per cent positive. Not even a complete pessimist – which she wasn't – could read anything negative into that. He hadn't responded before because he hadn't been on Facebook, he was pleased to hear from her, and he wanted; no *looked forward* to seeing her again. Win, win!

She dashed off a quick reply to let him know she looked forward to it too, and would be in touch when she got home. Then she got on with typing up her notes with a silly grin on her face. She had a date. Well, sort of. Maybe.

A while later, she'd finished her notes and had emailed them to herself for security. She'd back them up properly when she was home. Shutting the laptop lid with a satisfied sigh, Annalise rolled off the bed and grabbed her phone to see what the time was. She didn't have time to go for a swim – just as well as she could no longer be bothered – but a shower and a wander into town to check out the nightlife was definitely still on the cards. Damien's message had lifted her mood and her enthusiasm, so she looked forward to a night out. Naturally, she'd rather be *with* Damien on the night out, than just thinking about him, but if she played her cards right then she could end up going out with him, and soon.

A little while later, her one inch heels click-clicked her arrival in the hotel bar. There was no way she was going out in teetering six inch heels. Despite them being pretty much a fashion necessity, they just weren't her thing – she'd end up falling on her face and making a complete arse of herself. Annalise shuddered at the thought. She'd decided to drop in to the bar for a drink on her way out, and to say a quick hello to Andre. Walking up to the bar – which was much busier tonight than it had been last night – she nodded to Andre as he finished serving another customer. He greeted her with a broad smile.

'Hi Andre. Thanks again for today. I typed up my notes, and they're great. I'm really pleased with the information I have, and I appreciate your help.'

'No problem. I had a nice time.' Annalise could tell by the expression on his face that he meant it, and he really didn't harbour any ill will towards her. Thank goodness for that. She really didn't like to upset people, and Andre was such a nice guy that he didn't deserve it.

'Good, I did too. Anyway,' she piped up, changing the subject, 'can I have a quick vodka and coke, please? I'm going into the town to have something to eat and check out the nightlife.'

'You are not eating here?' Andre replied, moving to fix her drink. 'The restaurants are wonderful.'

'Not tonight. Tonight I explore the town, tomorrow I'll spend some time here checking out the facilities and restaurants. And the spa!'

Andre smiled and handed Annalise her drink. She raised her glass in thanks as he moved away to serve his next customer. Eager to get out and do some more exploring,

Annalise made short work of her vodka and coke, then gave a little wave to Andre as she left.

Annalise flopped onto the bed for the second time that day. Though by now it was growing very close to being the day after. She was ready for some shut eye, which she was sure would be upon her within seconds.

Annoyingly, it wasn't. She felt both physically and mentally exhausted and yet ten or so minutes later, she wasn't slipping into the blissful sleep she'd expected. Letting out what was now a thoroughly frustrated sigh, she tossed and turned, punched the pillows a little, then settled down again. Just as she thought she was growing closer to dreamland, an insistent throb began between her legs.

Oh, for fuck's sake! A solo session in the shower and an almost-encounter with a hunky barman isn't enough for you? Annalise mentally chastised her clit, which had reminded her of its presence at the most inappropriate time. Its only reply was a tingling sensation, a sure-fire indicator that there was blood headed to her lady bits in anticipation of some late-night fun.

Rolling her eyes, Annalise gave in to the arousal. It was pointless fighting it; it'd take her an age to get to sleep if she was horny, so she may as well give her suddenly insatiable libido what it wanted. If only she had her trusty *Rabbit*, then she could be racing towards climax in no time at all. Unfortunately, she would just have to make do with her hand and her overactive imagination.

Luckily, despite the late hour and her tiredness, Annalise's imagination was in fine form. Almost as soon as she'd tucked her right hand between her legs, her mind started supplying some mighty erotic images to help her on the road to orgasm. At first they were vague images of people in various states of undress and stages of naughtiness. Soon, though, Annalise's thoughts focussed, and the unknown faces and bodies disappeared, to be replaced with Damien's. They were together on the bench where she and Andre had had their moment – and would have done a lot more if it hadn't been for the inexplicable draw Annalise felt towards Damien, a guy she barely knew.

Annalise had no idea whether Damien would be the sort to screw in a public place – though the oft-used saying implicated the quiet ones – but she was quite happy to allow the fantasy to play out. In her mind, Damien was wearing the clothes he'd had on when she'd met him – hardly surprising as she'd never seen him in anything else – but his hair was loose. Fantasy Annalise had taken full advantage of this fact and had buried her hands in the curly mass, using it to tug his head back and expose his throat, which she was peppering with kisses and nibbles as she rocked herself to orgasm in his lap.

Meanwhile, real Annalise had increased the speed and ferocity at which she was teasing herself to climax. Her cunt had gone from damp and throbbing to slick, swollen and hungry, and now Annalise used her other hand to finger-fuck herself as she stroked and pinched her greedy clit. All the while she enjoyed the graphic images in her head as her body was lost to sensation.

As the scenario in her head became more heated, her physical movements became more frantic. Annalise's abdomen tightened, and the walls of her pussy contracted around her thrusting fingers. Pinpricks of arousal raced over and under her skin and gathered in her crotch. The delicious anticipation made her hold her breath as her fingers continued to play, then Annalise felt as though she was suspended, weightless. The feeling was fleeting, peaceful, and seconds later she was tumbling into an orgasm so powerful that white dots danced and swirled beneath her tightly-closed eyelids and her fantasy disappeared to be replaced by an overwhelming sensation of utter bliss.

As her orgasm abated, Annalise felt even more exhausted. Her limbs felt heavy, and she barely had the energy to pull her hands from where they were crammed between her legs and drop them, still wet with her juices, to the mattress at her sides. Regardless of her exhaustion, Annalise still felt well and truly satiated and she quickly fell asleep with a smile on her face, and thoughts of Damien filling her mind.

Chapter Seven

THIS WAS GOING TO be the time, she was sure of it. Annalise was so nervous and on edge she was sure that even if she didn't set the scanners off, the airport security staff would take one look at her and pull her into a room and snap on their rubber gloves. And that would really suck, because she had a date. Well, sort of.

It was two weeks after her trip to Portugal – and meeting Damien – and Annalise was back at the airport, flying out on another job. Despite the unspoken agreement that they would meet up again – and Annalise's promise to herself that she wouldn't be a wimp any more – it seemed neither of them was brave enough to actually set up a date to do it outside of the airport. Their increasingly frequent Facebook messages were full of chatter and banter, but no actual forward planning. Therefore, Annalise was mighty glad she didn't have long to wait for her short jaunt to Edinburgh, and the opportunity to swing by and see Damien. He knew her flight was today, so hopefully he'd be able to slope off for a break again.

In spite of her nerves, she got through airport security with no issues. Suddenly, she was even more nervous. There was nothing standing between her and Damien now. Physically, that was. Mentally and emotionally there were several hurdles the pair of them needed to vault if they were to ever get any further than coffee and muffins in the airport cafe. For what felt like the millionth time in the past couple of weeks, Annalise wished desperately she could speak to Tammy. Deep down, though, she knew exactly what her best friend would say:

"For God's sake, girl, if you like him, go for it! Don't wait for him to ask you out. You know how clueless blokes can be; he probably hasn't got the faintest idea that you like him in that way. Just ask him out. If he says no, which he won't if he's got any sense, then at least you'll know. But you'll never know if you don't try. Remember our mantra?"

Of course Annalise remembered the mantra. They'd stumbled across the phrase in their teens, and used it many times to explain away decisions galore; terrible boyfriends, awful hairstyles, dreadful clothes. As they got older, it had a much more sensible application; to give them the confidence to chase various opportunities, whether in life or love.

I'd rather regret something I did do, than something I didn't do.

It was a damn good mantra, and it had always stood Annalise in good stead in the past.

It was high time to bring that success into the present. Walking towards the bookshop, Annalise didn't falter or hesitate. She knew if she did, it was game over. If she wanted Damien, she was damn well going to have to get him. She imagined Tammy and Andre cheering her on, and felt a little braver.

She crossed the threshold, then slowed her pace. She may be about to ask him out, but she still wanted to be casual about it. Moving through the shop, she turned her head this way and that, as though deciding where to go and browse first. There was no sign of him.

Annalise did a full circuit of the shop before allowing herself to admit a disappointing defeat. She stood in the travel section where they'd first met and stared at the books on the shelves without really seeing them. She couldn't believe it. After coming to the airport way earlier than necessary, and psyching herself up to ask him out, he wasn't bloody there. Fucking typical. *I won't have the chance to regret or not regret if I can't even speak to him. This totally* sucks!

She was about to turn tail and leave the bookshop, when she heard someone coming into the store. Naturally, people enter shops all the time, but the amount of noise the person was making, coupled with the speed they were walking – people mooch in bookshops, not march – made Annalise suspect it wasn't a customer. As the noise grew closer and the figure passed by the end of the aisle, she realised she was right.

Damien stopped dead when he saw her, and a smile lit up his handsome face. Her heart rate increased and she had to mentally nudge herself to smile back before he thought something was wrong.

'Hey,' he said. 'Let me just go give this change to Cassie.' He indicated the cloth bag he was carrying, 'and I'll be right back.'

He walked off, the coins in the bag rattling with each step. In no time at all he re-joined Annalise in the travel aisle.

'Hey, I'm back,' he said, completely pointlessly. Annalise wondered if he was as nervous about seeing her again as she was him.

'Hey,' she said, 'I was beginning to think you'd pulled a sickie or something. Last time we spoke you said you were working today.'

'Nope, no sickie for me. I just went to get some change for the till. So, you all set for Bonnie Scotland?'

'I sure am. I have my wellies and an umbrella!'

He laughed.

'So …' Annalise said before she chickened out, 'Can I whisk you away to the cafe? There's a coffee and a muffin in there with your name on it.'

'Let me just check. It's quiet, so it shouldn't be a problem.'

He was back within a minute. 'I am free to be whisked away, ma'am. Bring on the coffee and muffins.'

So far, so good, thought Annalise. Now I just have to ask him out on a proper date.

They walked out of the shop and in the direction of the cafe.

'Muffins? How many am I buying you?'

'I am pretty hungry. And you didn't bring me a present back from Portugal.' He pouted for good measure.

Annalise laughed. 'Oh, I'm sorry. I didn't realise you wanted one. Perhaps I can make it up to you and get you some shortbread from Edinburgh?'

'Ooh,' he said, his pretend-sulk quickly forgotten, 'that would be nice. I love shortbread.'

'Why aren't I surprised? Your sweet tooth seems to be just as pronounced as mine.'

He grinned. 'What can I say? The worse it is for me, the more I seem to like it.'

'So how on earth do you stay so slim? You certainly don't look like you eat a lot of junk food.'

Damien shrugged. 'Dunno. Fast metabolism, I guess. I'm sure it'll catch up with me one day, and I'll have to start exercising daily just to stave off a heart attack.'

I can think of an exercise I'd like to do with you.

The thought had popped into her head, unbidden, but now as she walked with him just inches from her side, she couldn't seem to get rid of it. She'd been daydreaming about him for two weeks, so now that she was actually with him again, her hormones and nerves were wreaking havoc and threatening to turn her into a crazy person. She needed to get a grip, and fast.

She smiled politely and they continued in silence. At the cafe, Annalise retrieved her purse from her bag and said, 'Your turn to grab us a table. Do I need to ask what you're having?'

Grinning, Damien replied, 'No, I don't think you do.'

Without another word he walked off in the direction of an empty table. Annalise watched him go, shaking her head and wondering for the umpteenth time how a guy so completely not her type was tying her up in knots. Perhaps that was the point, she surmised. Some of her exes had been complete and utter arseholes. Others just hadn't been right for her. Somehow, Damien was totally different to all of them.

And she was going to ask him out. She was! She placed her order and waited patiently as the server put it together for her, then murmured her thanks.

Annalise stuffed her purse back into her bag and picked up the tray, heading towards the table Damien was sitting at. The mantra scrolled through her brain.

I'd rather regret something I did do, than something I didn't do.

I'd rather regret something I did do, than something I didn't do.

I'd rather regret something I did do, than something I didn't do.

'Here ya go,' she said, removing the items one by one from the tray and putting it on the spare seat next to her. 'Don't say I never buy you anything!'

Damien laughed. 'I was only joking about the muffins, plural.'

'Well, I'm not taking them back now,' Annalise scolded, 'so you'll just have to eat them, won't you?'

'We'll share.'

Annalise had her opening. It was now or never.

I'd rather regret something I did do, than something I didn't do.

Really, this was pathetic! She was a grown woman, for God's sake!

'Speaking of sharing,' she finally said, though the pause had been long enough to make Damien frown a little at her words, 'I was wondering if ... you might like to go to dinner with me? When I'm back from Edinburgh.'

Damien's eyes widened, and Annalise's heart plummeted. She dropped her gaze to the table. She'd fucked up. He didn't like her in that way, he was just being friendly. He ...

'I'd love to.'

She quickly looked back at his face, feeling decidedly more chipper as she saw the smile on it. Not to mention the dimple, which she was sure she'd find adorable for the rest of her days.

He looked suddenly uncomfortable, though, and Annalise felt her good mood dissipate. Fuck me, she thought, this conversation is like being on an emotional fucking rollercoaster.

'Although ...' his demeanour indicating that his words were a struggle, 'can I just clarify something? Do you mean dinner ... as in a date?'

Damn. He's not making this easy for me, is he? Despite all the hints to the contrary, Annalise couldn't help but think that perhaps Damien *didn't* want to be any more than friends. And she had already used up her quota of courage for the day. A straight *yes* was out of the question. Instead, she went with a slightly cowardly, 'Do you want it to be?'

Their eyes met, and Annalise's heart did that almost-painful pounding thing again as he pinned her to the spot with his intense gaze. His eyes gave her the answer she wanted, but it didn't stop her grinning like a fool when he finally said, 'Yes. I would like that. Very much.'

Chapter Eight

THE DOORBELL SOUNDED, AND Annalise let out a small shriek. Not because it had startled her or anything, but because ...

He's here. He's early. Fuckity-fuck-fuck!

Luckily she was ready. Damien's early appearance at her front door had merely interrupted her making sure every hair was in place, that there were no pieces of fluff or loose threads on her dress, that her stockings weren't laddered ...

Ding-dong!

Taking a deep breath, and feeling every inch like a teenager on her first ever date, Annalise padded down the stairs and to the front door. As a further delaying tactic, she slid the covering of the spy-hole to one side and looked through it. Yes, it was definitely Damien.

Well, who else were you expecting, you idiot?

She opened the door, and caught him halfway through his cute tucking-hair-behind-the-ears thing.

'Hi,' she said, stepping back, 'please come in. I just have to grab my shoes and bag, and I'm ready to go.'

'Hi,' he replied, moving into her hallway, 'there's no rush if you're not quite ready. Our reservation isn't until eight.'

'No, I'm ready. Honest.' She dashed back upstairs, pulled on her shoes and grabbed her bag. Then she returned to where Damien was still standing in the hall, an amused expression on his face.

'What's the matter?' she asked, nervously smoothing her hair, then her dress.

'Nothing. I just thought we'd got past the nervous thing, that's all.'

Since their conversation in the airport, when Annalise had finally bitten the bullet and asked Damien out, the dynamic between them had changed. They'd exchanged mobile telephone numbers and had sent seemingly endless text messages the entire time Annalise was in Edinburgh, and when she got home, too.

As a result, they'd managed to get past the whole shy, awkward, I'm-not-sure-if-you-like-me-or-not phase. Now they were both on the same page. Except that now Annalise knew for a fact that Damien liked her as more than a friend and had stopped worrying about rejection, she had a new problem.

'But what if I fuck it up?'

'Pardon?'

'I'm still nervous because now I'm worried that I'll fuck up what could potentially be a really good thing between us.'

Damien was silent for a few seconds, then he said, 'And what makes you think it'll be you that fucks things up? It could be me!'

He took a step towards her. He was now so close she could see her own solemn-looking face reflected in the lenses of his glasses.

'Alternatively, neither of us could fuck it up. Things could be great between us. Perfect, even. But …' He raised his eyebrows and fixed her with a stern stare, '… we'll never know unless we try, will we? Let's just operate on a policy of honesty and take each day as it comes, eh?'

Annalise couldn't argue with his logic, so she smiled and nodded. She started to move towards the front door to begin their first official date, when Damien grabbed her arm. She spun to face him.

'By the way,' he said, a hint of colour flushed across his cheeks, 'I just wanted to say, you look gorgeous tonight. Not that you don't always, but tonight ... well, you know what I mean!'

He dropped a quick kiss on Annalise's cheek then let go of her arm.

'I'll go and start the car while you're locking up.'

He opened the door and dashed out of it, leaving a very pleased and amused Annalise standing in the hallway, with a big grin on her face. She felt elated, excited and horny all at the same time, all because of a shy travel-and-chocolate-loving bookworm.

And pretty soon, she was going to find out whether there was any truth in the saying about it always being the quiet ones. She could hardly wait.

Pulling the door shut behind her, Annalise locked it and dropped her keys into the side pocket of her handbag, then made her way to where Damien's car idled on her driveway. Part of her expected him to jump out of the car and open the passenger door for her, but he didn't. She was glad. It may be a chivalrous gesture, but it was also seriously outdated. And besides, she had very little room for chivalry in her life. All she wanted was a guy to be her equal, her best friend and her lover. With each passing day, she was more and more convinced that Damien could be all of those things, and more.

She got in and glanced at him. He seemed to have got over his earlier embarrassment and gave a small smile as he waited patiently for her to shut the car door and fasten her seatbelt.

'Ready to hit the road?' he asked.

'Not quite,' Annalise replied, surprising herself. 'I just wanted to say something first.'

'Oh?'

'Yes. I just wanted to let you know that you look gorgeous tonight, too. I know you usually wear your hair up because of work, but it sure looks good loose.'

She wanted to end that sentence with *"and I'd love to*

tangle my fingers in it", but she managed to stop herself. They may both be on the same page, but she still didn't want to scare him off on their first date.

'Oh, uh ...' Clearly taken aback by Annalise's comment, he fiddled with his shirt cuffs for a second, then finally replied, 'Thanks.'

Perhaps I've taken the equality thing a little too far. I've embarrassed the poor guy again.

'So,' she said brightly, 'now that incredibly awkward conversation is out of the way, shall we go?'

Damien flashed her a grateful smile. The two of them made small talk for the 20 or so minutes it took them to get to the restaurant. It was a little out of the way, down a long country lane on the outskirts of a village near to the one they both lived in. Neither of them had been before, but a friend of Damien's had recommended it, so they'd decided to check it out.

'By the way,' Damien said as he steered the car into a space in the restaurant's car park, 'we're booked into the Brasserie restaurant. They had a fine dining option, too, but I suspected you might find it a little too fussy. I hope that's OK. I can try to change it, if you like.'

'Oh, God no,' Annalise replied. 'You suspected absolutely right. Don't get me wrong, I do appreciate a nice setting and good food – but I'd much rather feel comfortable in my surroundings. Not to mention be able to both pronounce the food on the menu!'

'And that's coming from someone who speaks several languages!'

They laughed, and their eyes met. Annalise could just about make out Damien's face in the light cast from a nearby streetlamp. Suddenly, his expression turned from mirthful to serious, and even in the near-darkness she was pinned to the spot by his gaze. Her pulse thrummed wildly in her throat, and butterflies took over her tummy. Seconds that felt like hours passed, and the sexual tension was such that you could have cut it with a knife, and yet ...

'Ready to go inside?'

Just like that, the spell of tension was broken. Annalise was gutted and grateful at the same time. Gutted because if it had gone on much longer, she'd have broken down and kissed him. Grateful because if she had kissed him, they probably never would have made it into the restaurant. And she was hungry.

Twenty or so minutes later, she was doubly grateful. They'd entered the restaurant, been greeted by an extremely attentive member of staff, and shown to their table. Once seated, their drinks order had been taken and they'd been presented with menus. And as much as Annalise fancied the pants off Damien and wanted to do unspeakable things to him, she now also wanted to sample each item off the menu. It all sounded delicious and she was having a tough time deciding.

Her eyes slid lower to the section headed "Desserts and Cheese". Damn. She'd have trouble deciding when it was time for dessert, too.

'What are you having?' Damien said from behind his menu, startling Annalise out of her food-induced state of distraction.

'I have no idea. It all sounds so good! And have you *seen* the desserts?'

'Of course I have. What do you take me for?'

They peeked at one another over the top of their menus. She could only see Damien's eyes, but she could tell he was smiling. She had an overwhelming urge to yank his menu from his hands and kiss the grin right off his face. Instead, she moved her menu so it hid her face and broke their eye contact.

For fuck's sake, this is ridiculous.

Annalise was torn. Part of her was enjoying the banter of their awkward flirtation, and the other part just wanted to end the almost-painful anticipation by dragging him to bed.

Immediately.

Suddenly, a thought sprung into her mind. Oh God. What if he doesn't want to have sex tonight? Maybe he believes in the third-date rule? Or even longer!

She gripped the menu so hard that she left little crescent moon indents on its surface. This was going to be the longest meal of her life.

Annalise put her spoon down and sat back in her chair with a satisfied groan. She retrieved the napkin from her lap and dabbed at her mouth. Damien, who'd already polished off his dessert, said, 'Nice?'

She indicated the empty bowl. 'What do you think?'

'I think it was probably just as delicious as mine, but I'll never know because you didn't offer me any to try.'

'Nor did you!'

'Maybe next time, eh?' He grinned at her.

The dull ache that had been between her legs for most of the evening blossomed into a throb that grew more powerful each second he looked at her. The sexual tension between them had been present since he'd walked in her door that night, ebbing and flowing dependent on what they were doing and saying. But now, with coffee the only possible reason for them to linger at the restaurant, the tension was almost at fever pitch.

A waitress approached the table to clear their places, and as she did so, she asked 'Can I get you anything else?'

Damien shot a questioning look at Annalise, who shook her head.

'No, thank you.'

'Just the bill then?'

'Yes please!' Damien and Annalise replied in unison, startling the waitress. She shot them a look and Annalise didn't miss the small smile that tugged at the corner of her mouth.

'Very well. I'll be right back.'

True to her word, the waitress was back quickly with their bill and a handheld credit card machine. Damien had his card out of his wallet and had handed it to the waitress before Annalise had even opened her handbag. She bit the inside of her mouth to keep from smiling.

Looks like he's just as eager to leave as I am. Thank fuck for that.

Less than five minutes later, they'd exited the restaurant and were getting back into Damien's car. As she fastened her seatbelt, the butterflies in Annalise's tummy came back with a vengeance.

'OK,' said Damien as he clipped his own seatbelt into place and started the car.

She waited for him to say something else, but he didn't. Another ominous silence hung between them. Annalise could have screamed. It was bloody obvious they were both thinking the same thing, so why couldn't one of them just *say something?!* They were adults, for God's sake. Why was it so difficult?

Finally, Damien broke the silence.

'So. My place or yours? I'm thinking yours, because it's a little closer, and I for one am dying to break this goddamn tension between us.'

An unexpected laugh escaped Annalise's mouth. 'I second that. Let's go.'

Shaking her head, she wondered if Damien's dessert had contained alcohol, making him suddenly so bold. It was either that, or his hormones were driving him crazy, just as hers were.

She didn't care either way, really. What mattered was the fact that the guy she'd been dreaming – and day-dreaming – about ever since she'd met him was taking her home. For sex. Maybe things were moving a little fast, but she could honestly say she'd never wanted a man – physically and emotionally – as much as she wanted Damien. It was incredibly cheesy, but she figured that if they were meant to be together, it wouldn't matter whether they went to bed on the first date or the hundredth.

Except perhaps he'd end up with blue balls, and she with whatever the female equivalent was …

Chapter Nine

THEY WERE SILENT AS Damien pulled on to Annalise's driveway. He killed the engine and they were both out of the car and at her front door in a matter of seconds. Annalise had already fished her keys out of her bag on the journey home, so there was only a small pause as she unlocked and opened the door.

Once they were inside, she locked the door behind them. When she turned, Damien was standing in the middle of her hallway fiddling with his shirt cuffs again.

'Uh-uh,' Annalise said, shaking her head at him, 'no more of that shy business. Please.'

He snapped his hands to his sides, looking suitably chastised. The dimple in his cheek appeared, along with a slight blush, when he said quietly, 'Upstairs?'

'Ohhh yes.'

Annalise dropped her handbag, kicked off her shoes and dashed up the stairs. Damien took off his shoes and followed closely behind her.

Flinging open the door to her bedroom, she snapped on the light, then crossed to the window and drew the curtains.

'We don't want to scare the neighbours now, do–'

Turning from the window, her words were cut off by Damien standing right in front of her. Annalise took a tiny step forward, and they were touching. She thrilled at the sensation of his body heat, and couldn't wait to feel the same heat, yet skin to skin. Sucking in a deep breath, she almost drooled at the scent. She could smell a mixture of shampoo and cologne, and it was *good*.

There was some tacit agreement that they'd now passed the point of no return – despite still being fully clothed – as Damien put his hands on Annalise's hips and pulled her more tightly to him. He said just one word before leaning down and capturing her mouth in a kiss.

'Condoms?'

The plural hadn't been lost on her, and the frisson of heat between her legs sparked into a full flame. *Fuuuuuuuuck.*

'Mmm-hmm ...' she replied, twining her arms around his neck and kissing him back. He was a damn good kisser. He had just the right mixture of confidence and skill, which made the butterflies in her tummy transform into crazy zings of lust and zoom wildly throughout her body.

The delicious feelings increased tenfold when Damien opened his lips and she felt his tongue try for access to her mouth. She gladly admitted it, and the hot caress of his tongue against hers caused a trickle of juices to slide from her pussy and soak into the gusset of her pants.

She was suddenly very glad she'd gone with her earlier instinct and worn not only matching, but very sexy lingerie. Not that she was going to be wearing it for much longer ...

Annalise shuffled forwards, gently pushing him. Damien took the hint and they moved as one towards her bed, falling onto it with her on top. Just as she leaned down to kiss him again, he stopped her. Removing his glasses, he gave a wicked smile and asked her to put them down on her bedside table.

'Don't want them getting in the way, do we?'

Climbing off him, Annalise carefully deposited his glasses on the bedside table. Then, agreeing with Damien's logic about things getting in the way, she quickly removed her earrings, necklace and bracelet. Finally, she opened her top drawer and retrieved a condom. Turning to face him once more, she saw that he'd moved so he was now positioned with his head on the pillows, and his hands behind his head, waiting. He raised his eyebrows.

'Oh, I'm sorry,' Annalise said, her voice dripping with sarcasm, 'was I taking too long?'

'Yes,' Damien replied without hesitation. 'Now come here.'

Annalise clambered across the bed and straddled Damien. She felt the bulge in his trousers pressing against her arse and wriggled against it. Dropping the condom on his chest, she said, 'I think you're going to be needing that.'

'You think?'

'Shut up and give me a kiss.'

'With pleasure, ma'am.'

Grabbing the condom packet in one hand, he reached up with the other and pulled her down on to him. Annalise opened her mouth immediately, eager to have his tongue in her mouth. Not to mention certain other places.

Shifting slightly, she transferred her weight from her hands to her elbows. Her breasts were crushed tight against his chest, causing them both to moan at the sensation. It was nice, but it hadn't been Annalise's end game. No, she'd freed her hands so she could do what she'd been longing to do for a very long time.

She tangled them in his hair. It felt every bit as good as she'd imagined; springy yet soft. Annalise had to restrain herself from yanking on it and getting to work on his exposed throat, like she had in one of her daydreams.

Maybe later.

For now, she was going to hold on tight and enjoy the ride.

Their kiss grew more heated, and Annalise's hips rocked almost involuntarily with every sensual slip and slide of their tongues. Of course, each and every movement was grinding her clit against Damien's erection, making them both more and more frenzied. Their tongues clashed increasingly violently, and Damien jerked beneath her, pushing his hard cock more forcefully against Annalise's vulva.

She growled, and thrust back. By now, she could feel her sodden knickers clinging to her pussy and could think of little else but Damien fucking her.

Sitting up suddenly, Annalise didn't bother to answer Damien's confused, 'What's up?' She thought her actions would make her intentions perfectly clear. Too impatient to turn around and get Damien to undo the zip, she grabbed the hem of her dress and tugged it over her head, dropping it to the floor beside the bed.

Damien didn't say another word. He didn't need to. His face said it all, as his gaze caressed her body; from her tousled hair down to where her crotch was pressed against his. She didn't think it was possible, but the more he stared the more aroused she became, until her stiffened nipples were chafing almost painfully against the cups of her lacy bra and her cunt felt like molten lava.

Annalise couldn't take it any more. Without a word, she reached down and undid the belt of his trousers. She tried to pull it from the loops, but because she was still astride him, he struggled to raise his bottom enough to help get rid of the belt.

Huffing impatiently, Annalise rolled off Damien and flopped down beside him. 'Get them off,' she said crossly.

He laughed, but did as he was told. 'Horny, are we?'

'What do you think?'

Damien stood up, then took off his trousers and socks. Now it was Annalise's turn to stare as he undid his shirt and dropped it to the floor with his other clothes. To be fair, she was so horny that he could have had a tattoo saying "MUM" emblazoned across his chest and she still would have wanted him, but there was no such atrocity. He was just as gorgeous shirtless as he was clothed. More so, actually.

He was definitely not what you would call muscular, but he was lithe and defined, and ... delicious. Annalise's gaze followed the trail of hair from his chest, down his torso and to where it disappeared into his boxer shorts, which were currently straining against a very eager erection.

Damien watched her watching him, and when her gaze flicked back to his face, he quirked an eyebrow and said, 'Will I do?'

Grinning, she said nothing, retrieving the condom from where it had been abandoned on the duvet and tossing it to him.

'You'll be needing that. Now.'

Damien gave a mock salute and slipped out of his boxer shorts, then tore open the condom packet. Annalise tried not to stare as he put it on, but she couldn't stop herself. His long fingers carefully eased the latex down his length and Annalise felt a fresh jolt of desire rush to her pussy.

Dropping onto her back, Annalise lifted her bottom, hooked her thumbs into the sides of her thong and shimmied out of it. She flicked one foot and sent it sailing across the room, then sat up, unhooked her bra and sent it in the same direction. She was just about to grab the top of one of her hold-up stockings to roll it off when Damien got back onto the bed and crawled over to her.

'Don't,' he said quietly, pushing her onto her back once more, 'leave them on.'

'Ooh,' she replied, shuffling backwards up the bed so her head was on the pillows, 'like them, do we?'

'What do you think?' he shot back, stroking his stiff cock a couple of times before moving between her legs and nudging them apart with his own.

It wasn't at all cool in the room, but as her pussy was exposed to the air, it certainly felt it. She didn't have long to think about how hot her pussy must be to feel that way because milliseconds later, Damien's hand was there, slipping between her parted labia and dipping into her wetness.

A deep moan came from Damien's throat as he touched her. Annalise's cunt clenched in response.

'You're so wet. Fuck, Annalise ... I want ...'

'I know, so do I. Please, do it now.'

'But don't you want ...'

'Later. There's time for that later. Please, just fuck me. Trust me, I'm so turned on that I'll have no trouble at all coming.'

A small smile crept onto his face. 'Really?'

'Really. Now come here.'

Damien covered her body with his, resting his weight on his knees and elbows, and looked into Annalise's eyes. Then, cupping her cheek with one hand, he lowered his face to hers and kissed her. Opening her mouth, she allowed him to thrust his tongue inside. This time, though, she caught it between her lips and sucked, pulling it deeper. A strangled moan came from Damien's throat, and Annalise felt his cock twitch against her vulva. She angled her hips, desperate to have him inside her.

It didn't quite work, but Damien was obviously just as eager to be inside her, as he removed his hand from her face and slipped it between their bodies. Grasping his cock, he pressed it against her entrance, then removed his hand.

Annalise was so wet and ready that with one thrust of Damien's hips he was balls-deep inside her. She forgot all about sucking his tongue, threw her head back and moaned loudly. They were still for a beat, then a minute movement from Damien had Annalise clasping her ankles around the back of his legs and gripping his arse in her hands.

'Damien, please. I am so desperate to come that it may get violent. Give me what you've got. We have a box of twelve condoms and all weekend.'

Damien chuckled. 'Just twelve? What do you take me for?'

A playful slap of his arse made him yelp. 'Shut up and fuck me.'

'Yes ma'am.'

She waited with insane anticipation as Damien raised himself up on his hands, and watched as he bent his head to look down at where their bodies were joined. Then he began to roll his hips, slowly. Too slowly. Digging her nails into his pert arse, she pulled him deeper, urging him on. 'Faster, harder. Please.'

She was whining with desperation. Damien picked up his pace, and the room was filled with the wet, slurping sound of her pussy being pounded, and their bodies slapping together. Annalise jerked her hips to meet him, thrust for thrust, and their moans and groans became more frequent and frenzied as they grew closer to orgasm.

Drawing in a deep breath, Annalise suddenly said, 'Damien.'

He took one look at her face, and nodded in understanding. Gritting his teeth, he pistoned his cock in and out of Annalise as she clung on to him for dear life, still meeting him, thrust for thrust.

Soon, Annalise felt tingles in her abdomen. Her pussy tightened around Damien's shaft, causing him to moan.

'Unh,' he gasped, 'I'm gonna come.'

'Do it.'

Annalise squeezed her eyes shut, revelling in the feeling of Damien's cock inside her, and the way his buttocks tensed and tightened beneath her hands. She sucked in a harsh breath as the tingles in her abdomen increased, and she tensed all over as she teetered on the very edge of her climax. A couple more thrusts from Damien, his pubic bone grinding into hers, and she was lost.

A squeal escaped her mouth, and she arched off the bed, the delicious sensations racing through every nerve ending and causing spots and strange patterns to dance and swirl before her eyes. Her pussy grasped and spasmed around Damien's shaft, causing him to grunt and growl. Then he suddenly froze, and let out a long, urgent moan. Milliseconds later, his cock started to twitch and jump inside her, shooting his load into the condom. Annalise simply held him tightly, feeling the waves of her orgasm start to ebb away, just as he started to relax and soften inside her.

Damien dropped down onto his elbows again and gave Annalise a long, heartfelt, toe-curlingly delicious kiss before gently rolling off her. Slipping an arm beneath her neck, he pulled her so her head was on his chest, where she rested happily. She smiled as she listened to his heart pounding in his chest – as no doubt hers still was – and the grin grew wider as Damien broke the silence by summing up her exact thoughts in one, not particularly eloquent, sentence.

'Fuck me, that was incredible.'

Annalise managed a heartfelt 'Mmm-hmm,' before she gave in to the heaviness of her eyelids.

Chapter Ten

A HORRIBLE NOISE DRAGGED Annalise out of a sleep which almost rivalled that of the dead.

'Unh?'

As she struggled to full consciousness, she became aware of the warm body spooning her. A glance over her shoulder at Damien made thoughts and memories of last night come crashing back into her mind. She grinned dopily, until the phone rang again.

'Oh for fuck's sake!'

She slipped out of Damien's grasp and shuffled across the bed until she could reach the phone on her nightstand. She pressed the button without bothering the check the caller ID.

'This had better be good.'

'Annalise?'

'Mum?'

'Are you ill, dear? Only you don't usually answer the telephone in that manner. Especially not at 11 a.m. on a Saturday morning.'

'Oh,' she said, a glance at the clock confirming it was indeed getting on for lunchtime, 'sorry, Mum. I just had a late night, that's all.'

A snigger from behind her alerted Annalise to the fact that Damien had woken up. She turned to face him, a finger to her lips.

'I see. Well, I'm just calling to make sure you're still OK for this evening.'

'This evening?'

Her mother sighed. 'Oh for goodness sake, Annalise. Are you sure you're all right? It's not like you to forget family arrangements. It's your father's birthday, remember.'

'Of course I remembered, Mum. I'm just half asleep, I didn't realise what the date was.'

'Hmph. Well, that's what happens when you lounge around in bed all day like some kind of sloth. It's no wonder you can't meet a man if your time is divided between work and sleep. You need some leisure time, dear. Perhaps we'd better find someone to pair you up with for tonight. I'll ring around, and see who we can rustle up. I can't see my only daughter being left on the shelf ...'

Annalise cut into her mother's sentence with a retort she knew would render her speechless. For a couple of seconds, at least. 'Actually, Mum, I'm bringing someone. His name is Damien and he's really looking forward to meeting you all. See you then. Bye.'

She put the phone down before her mother could respond. Rolling over on the bed to face Damien, she cringed and covered her face with her hands.

'Argh! I can't believe I just said that. I'll have to call her back in a minute and make an excuse. I can't subject you to that. We haven't been together five minutes.'

Damien took her wrists and pulled them away to reveal her face.

'It's all right. I'll go.'

'Are you serious?! You're volunteering to meet my family? After one night with me?'

'Well,' he said, entwining his fingers with hers, 'I'm kind of hoping I'm going to be more than a one-night stand, so why not? I've got to meet them sooner or later, so it may as well be tonight.'

'Well, I won't hold it against you if you run away and never come back when you've met them. They're pretty full on. You'll get the whole works. By the end of the night, Aunty Pam will have demanded the names of our unborn

214

children. Do you really know what you're letting yourself in for?'

He shrugged. 'I haven't told you about my family yet. For all you know, they could be even worse.'

'True. But we did agree to take each day as it comes. So, my family today, yours tomorrow, then the rest of the week in bed?'

Damien rolled on the bed, pulling Annalise on top of him. She felt his rapidly stiffening cock pressing against her bottom, and grinned.

Grinning back, Damien said, 'I've got a better idea.'

'Oh yeah? What's that?'

'How about more bed, then your family, then my family, then more bed?'

Reaching behind her to stroke his now fully-awakened dick, Annalise laughed and said, 'Sounds like a plan to me!'

More great titles in
The Secret Library

Traded Innocence
9781908262028

One Long Hot Summer
9781908262066

The Thousand and One Nights
9781908262080

The Game
9781908262103

Hungarian Rhapsody
9781908262127

The Game – Jeff Cott

The Game is the story of Ellie's bid to change from sexy, biddable housewife to sexy dominant goddess.

Ellie and Jake are a happily married couple who play a bedroom game. Having lost the last Game Ellie must start the new one where she left off – bound and gagged on the bed. As she figures out how to tie herself up before Jake's return from work, Ellie remembers the last Game and has ideas for the new one. Jake is immensely strong and loving and has seemingly endless sexual stamina so the chances of Ellie truly gaining control look slim. Although she has won the Game on occasions, she suspects he lets her win just so he can overwhelm her in the next. She has to find a way to break this pattern.

But does she succeed?

One of Us – Antonia Adams

Successful artist Natalie Crane is midway through a summer exhibition with friend and agent Anton when Will Falcon strolls tantalisingly into her life. After a messy divorce, a relationship is not Natalie's priority. Anton takes an immediate dislike to the shaven-headed composer, but Natalie is captivated. He is everything she is not: free, impulsive and seemingly with no thought for the future. He introduces her to Dorset's beautiful coves and stunning countryside and their time together is magical.

Things get complicated when her most famous painting, a nude self-portrait, is stolen and there are no signs of a break-in. When it's time for her return to London, Will doesn't turn up to say goodbye, and she cannot trace him. Anton tells her to forget him, but she cannot. Then she discovers the stakes are much higher than they first appeared.

Taste It – Sommer Marsden

Jill and Cole are competing for the title of *Best Chef*. The spicy, sizzling and heated televised contest fuels a lust in Jill she'd rather keep buried. She can't be staring at the man's muscles ... he's her competition! During a quick cooking throwdown things start to simmer and it becomes harder and harder for Jill to ignore that she's smitten in the kitchen. Cole's suggestive glances and sly smiles aren't helping her any. When fate puts her in his shower and then his chivalrous nature puts her in his borrowed clothes, there's no way to deny the natural heat between them.

One Long Hot Summer – Elizabeth Coldwell

Lily's looking after her friend, Amanda's, home on the Dorset coast, hoping it will ease her writer's block and help her get over her ex, Alex. What she doesn't expect is that Amanda's 21-year-old son Ryan will arrive at the house, planning to spend the summer surfing and partying – or that he'll have grown up quite so nicely. Ryan's as attracted to her as she is to him – but surely acting on her feelings for a man 14 years her junior is inappropriate? And when Alex makes a sudden reappearance in her life, wanting to get back together, should she follow her head or her heart? How can she resolve this case of summer madness?

Just Another Lady – Penelope Friday

Regency lady Elinor has fallen on hard times. The death of her father and the entail of their house put Elinor and her mother in difficulty; and her mother's illness has brought doctor's bills that they cannot pay. Lucius Crozier was Elinor's childhood friend and adversary; and there has always been a spark of attraction between the pair. Now renowned as a womaniser, he offers a marriage of convenience (for him!) in return for the payment of Elinor's mother's medical bills. Reluctantly, she agrees. But Lucius has made enemies of other gentlemen of the upper echelon by playing fast and loose with their mistresses, and one man is determined to take his revenge through Lucius's new wife ...

Safe Haven – Shanna Germain

Kallie Peters has finally made her dream come true – she's turned the family farm into Safe Haven, an animal sanctuary. But financial woes are pressing in on her, and she's worried that the only way to keep the farm is to allow her rich ex-boyfriend back into her life. When a sexy stranger shows up in her driveway with a wiggling puppy in his arms, she knows it's her chance for a hot rendezvous before she gives up her freedom.

The sex is hot, wild and passionate – the perfect interim before returning to the pressures of real life – but something else is happening between them. Can they find a way to save their dreams, their passions and their hearts, or will they have to say goodbye to all they've come to love?